J.R.R.Tolkien.

J.R.R. TOLKIEN

THE LORD OF THE RINGS
comprising:

BOOK ONE
THE RING SETS OUT

BOOK TWO
THE RING GOES SOUTH

BOOK THREE
THE TREASON OF ISENGARD

BOOK FOUR
THE RING GOES EAST

BOOK FIVE
THE WAR OF THE RING

BOOK SIX
THE END OF THE THIRD AGE

and

APPENDICES

THE RING
GOES EAST

BEING THE FOURTH BOOK OF
THE LORD OF THE RINGS

BY

J.R.R. TOLKIEN

An imprint of HarperCollinsPublishers

First published in Great Britain by
George Allen & Unwin 1954
Second edition 1966
This new reset edition published by
HarperCollins*Publishers* 1994
First published in seven volumes 1999
This seven-volume edition 2001

3 5 7 9 10 8 6 4

Collins is an imprint of HarperCollins*Publishers* Ltd,
77–85 Fulham Palace Road, Hammersmith, London w6 8jb

The HarperCollins website address is
www.**fire**and**water**.com

 ® is a registered trademark of
The J.R.R. Tolkien Estate Limited

www.tolkien.co.uk

ISBN 0 00 763558 3

Printed and bound in Great Britain by
Omnia Books Limited, Glasgow

CONTENTS

Three Rings for the Elven-kings under the sky,
  Seven for the Dwarf-lords in their halls of stone,
Nine for Mortal Men doomed to die,
  One for the Dark Lord on his dark throne
In the Land of Mordor where the Shadows lie.
    One Ring to rule them all, One Ring to find them,
    One Ring to bring them all and in the darkness bind them
In the Land of Mordor where the Shadows lie.

CHAPTER I

THE TAMING OF SMÉAGOL

'Well, master, we're in a fix and no mistake,' said Sam Gamgee. He stood despondently with hunched shoulders beside Frodo, and peered out with puckered eyes into the gloom.

It was the third evening since they had fled from the Company, as far as they could tell: they had almost lost count of the hours during which they had climbed and laboured among the barren slopes and stones of the Emyn Muil, sometimes retracing their steps because they could find no way forward, sometimes discovering that they had wandered in a circle back to where they had been hours before. Yet on the whole they had worked steadily eastward, keeping as near as they could find a way to the outer edge of this strange twisted knot of hills. But always they found its outward faces sheer, high and impassable, frowning over the plain below; beyond its tumbled skirts lay livid festering marshes where nothing moved and not even a bird was to be seen.

The hobbits stood now on the brink of a tall cliff, bare and bleak, its feet wrapped in mist; and behind them rose the broken highlands crowned with drifting cloud. A chill wind blew from the East. Night was gathering over the shapeless lands before them; the sickly green of them was fading to a sullen brown. Far away to the right the Anduin, that had gleamed fitfully in sun-breaks during the day, was now hidden in shadow. But their eyes did not look beyond the River, back to Gondor, to their friends, to the lands of Men. South and east they stared to where, at the edge of the oncoming night, a dark line hung, like distant mountains of motionless smoke. Every now and again a tiny red gleam far away flickered upwards on the rim of earth and sky.

'What a fix!' said Sam. 'That's the one place in all the lands we've ever heard of that we don't want to see any closer; and that's the one place we're trying to get to! And that's just where we can't get, nohow. We've come the wrong way altogether, seemingly. We can't get down; and if we did get down, we'd find all that green land a nasty bog, I'll warrant. Phew! Can you smell it?' He sniffed at the wind.

'Yes, I can smell it,' said Frodo, but he did not move, and his eyes remained fixed, staring out towards the dark line and the flickering flame. 'Mordor!' he muttered under his breath. 'If I must go there, I wish I could come there quickly and make an end!' He shuddered. The wind was chilly and yet heavy with an odour of cold decay. 'Well,' he said, at last withdrawing his eyes, 'we cannot stay here all night, fix or no fix. We must find a more sheltered spot, and camp once more; and perhaps another day will show us a path.'

'Or another and another and another,' muttered Sam. 'Or maybe no day. We've come the wrong way.'

'I wonder,' said Frodo. 'It's my doom, I think, to go to that Shadow yonder, so that a way will be found. But will good or evil show it to me? What hope we had was in speed. Delay plays into the Enemy's hands – and here I am: delayed. Is it the will of the Dark Tower that steers us? All my choices have proved ill. I should have left the Company long before, and come down from the North, east of the River and of the Emyn Muil, and so over the hard of Battle Plain to the passes of Mordor. But now it isn't possible for you and me alone to find a way back, and the Orcs are prowling on the east bank. Every day that passes is a precious day lost. I am tired, Sam. I don't know what is to be done. What food have we got left?'

'Only those, what d'you call 'em, *lembas*, Mr. Frodo. A fair supply. But they are better than naught, by a long bite. I never thought, though, when I first set tooth in them, that I should ever come to wish for a change. But I do now: a bit of plain bread, and a mug – aye, half a mug – of beer would go down proper. I've lugged my cooking-gear all the way from the last camp, and what use has it been? Naught to make a fire with, for a start; and naught to cook, not even grass!'

They turned away and went down into a stony hollow. The westering sun was caught into clouds, and night came swiftly. They slept as well as they could for the cold, turn and turn about, in a nook among great jagged pinnacles of weathered rock; at least they were sheltered from the easterly wind.

'Did you see them again, Mr. Frodo?' asked Sam, as they sat, stiff and chilled, munching wafers of *lembas*, in the cold grey of early morning.

'No,' said Frodo. 'I've heard nothing, and seen nothing, for two nights now.'

'Nor me,' said Sam. 'Grrr! Those eyes did give me a turn! But perhaps we've shaken him off at last, the miserable slinker. Gollum! I'll give him *gollum* in his throat, if ever I get my hands on his neck.'

'I hope you'll never need to,' said Frodo. 'I don't know how he followed us; but it may be that he's lost us again, as you say. In this dry bleak land we can't leave many footprints, nor much scent, even for his snuffling nose.'

'I hope that's the way of it,' said Sam. 'I wish we could be rid of him for good!'

'So do I,' said Frodo; 'but he's not my chief trouble. I wish we could get away from these hills! I hate them. I feel all naked on the east side, stuck up here with nothing but the dead flats between me and that Shadow yonder. There's an Eye in it. Come on! We've got to get down today somehow.'

But that day wore on, and when afternoon faded towards evening they were still scrambling along the ridge and had found no way of escape.

Sometimes in the silence of that barren country they fancied that they heard faint sounds behind them, a stone falling, or the imagined step of flapping feet on the rock. But if they halted and stood still listening, they heard no more, nothing but the wind sighing over the edges of the stones – yet even that reminded them of breath softly hissing through sharp teeth.

All that day the outer ridge of the Emyn Muil had been bending gradually northward, as they struggled on. Along its brink there now stretched a wide tumbled flat of scored and weathered rock, cut every now and again by trench-like gullies that sloped steeply down to deep notches in the cliff-face. To find a path in these clefts, which were becoming deeper and more frequent, Frodo and Sam were driven to their left, well away from the edge, and they did not notice that for several miles they had been going slowly but steadily downhill: the cliff-top was sinking towards the level of the lowlands.

At last they were brought to a halt. The ridge took a sharper bend northward and was gashed by a deeper ravine. On the further side it reared up again, many fathoms at a single leap: a great grey cliff loomed before them, cut sheer down as if by a knife stroke. They could go no further forwards, and must turn now either west or east. But west would lead them only into more labour and delay, back towards the heart of the hills; east would take them to the outer precipice.

'There's nothing for it but to scramble down this gully, Sam,' said Frodo. 'Let's see what it leads to!'

'A nasty drop, I'll bet,' said Sam.

The cleft was longer and deeper than it seemed. Some way down they found a few gnarled and stunted trees, the first they had seen for days: twisted birch for the most part, with here and there a fir-tree. Many were dead and gaunt, bitten to the core by the eastern winds. Once in milder days there must have been a fair thicket in the ravine, but now, after some fifty yards, the trees came to an end, though old broken stumps straggled on almost to the cliff's brink. The bottom of the gully, which lay along the edge of a rock-fault, was rough with broken stone and slanted steeply down. When they came at last to the end of it, Frodo stooped and leaned out.

'Look!' he said. 'We must have come down a long way, or else the cliff has sunk. It's much lower here than it was, and it looks easier too.'

Sam knelt beside him and peered reluctantly over the edge. Then he glanced up at the great cliff rising up, away on their left. 'Easier!' he grunted. 'Well, I suppose it's always easier getting down than up. Those as can't fly can jump!'

'It would be a big jump still,' said Frodo. 'About, well' – he stood for a moment measuring it with his eyes – 'about eighteen fathoms, I should guess. Not more.'

'And that's enough!' said Sam. 'Ugh! How I do hate looking down from a height! But looking's better than climbing.'

'All the same,' said Frodo, 'I think we could climb here; and I think we shall have to try. See – the rock is quite different from what it was a few miles back. It has slipped and cracked.'

The outer fall was indeed no longer sheer, but sloped outwards a little. It looked like a great rampart or sea-wall whose foundations had shifted, so that its courses were all twisted and disordered, leaving great fissures and long slanting edges that were in places almost as wide as stairs.

'And if we're going to try and get down, we had better try at once. It's getting dark early. I think there's a storm coming.'

The smoky blur of the mountains in the East was lost in a deeper blackness that was already reaching out westwards with long arms. There was a distant mutter of thunder borne on the rising breeze. Frodo sniffed the air and looked up doubtfully at the sky. He strapped his belt outside his cloak and tightened it, and settled his light pack on his back; then he stepped towards the edge. 'I'm going to try it,' he said.

'Very good!' said Sam gloomily. 'But I'm going first.'

'You?' said Frodo. 'What's made you change your mind about climbing?'

'I haven't changed my mind. But it's only sense: put the one lowest as is most likely to slip. I don't want to come down : top of you and knock you off – no sense in killing two with one fall.'

Before Frodo could stop him, he sat down, swung his legs over the brink, and twisted round, scrabbling with his toes for a foothold. It is doubtful if he ever did anything braver in cold blood, or more unwise.

'No, no! Sam, you old ass!' said Frodo. 'You'll kill yourself for certain, going over like that without even a look to see what to make for. Come back!' He took Sam under the armpits and hauled him up again. 'Now, wait a bit and be patient!' he said. Then he lay on the ground, leaning out and looking down; but the light seemed to be fading quickly, although the sun had not yet set. 'I think we could manage this,' he said presently. 'I could at any rate; and you could too, if you kept your head and followed me carefully.'

'I don't know how you can be so sure,' said Sam. 'Why! You can't see to the bottom in this light. What if you comes to a place where there's nowhere to put your feet or your hands?'

'Climb back, I suppose,' said Frodo.

'Easy said,' objected Sam. 'Better wait till morning and more light.'

'No! Not if I can help it,' said Frodo with a sudden strange vehemence. 'I grudge every hour, every minute. I'm going down to try it out. Don't you follow till I come back or call!'

Gripping the stony lip of the fall with his fingers he let himself gently down, until when his arms were almost at full stretch, his toes found a ledge. 'One step down!' he said. 'And this ledge broadens out to the right. I could stand there without a hold. I'll——' his words were cut short.

The hurrying darkness, now gathering great speed, rushed up from the East and swallowed the sky. There was a dry splitting crack of thunder right overhead. Searing lightning smote down into the hills. Then came a blast of savage wind, and with it, mingling with its roar, there came a high shrill shriek. The hobbits had heard just such a cry far away in the

Marish as they fled from Hobbiton, and even there in the woods of the Shire it had frozen their blood. Out here in the waste its terror was far greater: it pierced them with cold blades of horror and despair, stopping heart and breath. Sam fell flat on his face. Involuntarily Frodo loosed his hold and put his hands over his head and ears. He swayed, slipped, and slithered downwards with a wailing cry.

Sam heard him and crawled with an effort to the edge. 'Master, master!' he called. 'Master!'

He heard no answer. He found he was shaking all over, but he gathered his breath, and once again he shouted: 'Master!' The wind seemed to blow his voice back into his throat, but as it passed, roaring up the gully and away over the hills, a faint answering cry came to his ears:

'All right, all right! I'm here. But I can't see.'

Frodo was calling with a weak voice. He was not actually very far away. He had slid and not fallen, and had come up with a jolt to his feet on a wider ledge not many yards lower down. Fortunately the rock-face at this point leaned well back and the wind had pressed him against the cliff, so that he had not toppled over. He steadied himself a little, laying his face against the cold stone, feeling his heart pounding. But either the darkness had grown complete, or else his eyes had lost their sight. All was black about him. He wondered if he had been struck blind. He took a deep breath.

'Come back! Come back!' he heard Sam's voice out of the blackness above.

'I can't,' he said. 'I can't see. I can't find any hold. I can't move yet.'

'What can I do, Mr. Frodo? What can I do?' shouted Sam, leaning out dangerously far. Why could not his master see? It was dim, certainly, but not as dark as all that. He could see Frodo below him, a grey forlorn figure splayed against the cliff. But he was far out of the reach of any helping hand.

There was another crack of thunder; and then the rain came. In a blinding sheet, mingled with hail, it drove against the cliff, bitter cold.

'I'm coming down to you,' shouted Sam, though how he hoped to help in that way he could not have said.

'No, no! wait!' Frodo called back, more strongly now. 'I shall be better soon. I feel better already. Wait! You can't do anything without a rope.'

'Rope!' cried Sam, talking wildly to himself in his excitement and relief. 'Well, if I don't deserve to be hung on the end of one as a warning to numbskulls! You're nowt but a ninnyhammer, Sam Gamgee: that's what the Gaffer said to me often enough, it being a word of his. Rope!'

'Stop chattering!' cried Frodo, now recovered enough to feel both amused and annoyed. 'Never mind your Gaffer! Are you trying to tell yourself you've got some rope in your pocket? If so, out with it!'

'Yes, Mr. Frodo, in my pack and all. Carried it hundreds of miles, and I'd clean forgotten it!'

'Then get busy and let an end down!'

Quickly Sam unslung his pack and rummaged in it. There indeed at the bottom was a coil of the silken-grey rope made by the folk of Lórien. He cast an end to his master. The darkness seemed to lift from Frodo's eyes, or else his sight was returning. He could see the grey line as it came dangling down, and he thought it had a faint silver sheen. Now that he had some point in the darkness to fix his eyes on, he felt less giddy. Leaning his weight forward, he made the end fast round his waist, and then he grasped the line with both hands.

Sam stepped back and braced his feet against a stump a yard or two from the edge. Half hauled, half scrambling, Frodo came up and threw himself on the ground.

Thunder growled and rumbled in the distance, and the rain was still falling heavily. The hobbits crawled away back into the gully; but they did not find much shelter there. Rills of water began to run down; soon they grew to a spate that splashed and fumed on the stones, and spouted out over the cliff like the gutters of a vast roof.

'I should have been half drowned down there, or washed

clean off,' said Frodo. 'What a piece of luck you had that rope!'

'Better luck if I'd thought of it sooner,' said Sam. 'Maybe you remember them putting the ropes in the boats, as we started off: in the elvish country. I took a fancy to it, and I stowed a coil in my pack. Years ago, it seems. "It may be a help in many needs," he said: Haldir, or one of those folk. And he spoke right.'

'A pity I didn't think of bringing another length,' said Frodo; 'but I left the Company in such a hurry and confusion. If only we had enough we could use it to get down. How long is your rope, I wonder?'

Sam paid it out slowly, measuring it with his arms: 'Five, ten, twenty, thirty ells, more or less,' he said.

'Who'd have thought it!' Frodo exclaimed.

'Ah! Who would?' said Sam. 'Elves are wonderful folk. It looks a bit thin, but it's tough; and soft as milk to the hand. Packs close too, and as light as light. Wonderful folk to be sure!'

'Thirty ells!' said Frodo considering. 'I believe it would be enough. If the storm passes before nightfall, I'm going to try it.'

'The rain's nearly given over already,' said Sam; 'but don't you go doing anything risky in the dim again, Mr. Frodo! And I haven't got over that shriek on the wind yet, if you have. Like a Black Rider it sounded – but one up in the air, if they can fly. I'm thinking we'd best lay up in this crack till night's over.'

'And I'm thinking that I won't spend a moment longer than I need, stuck up on this edge with the eyes of the Dark Country looking over the marshes,' said Frodo.

With that he stood up and went down to the bottom of the gully again. He looked out. Clear sky was growing in the East once more. The skirts of the storm were lifting, ragged and wet, and the main battle had passed to spread its great wings over the Emyn Muil, upon which the dark thought of Sauron brooded for a while. Thence it turned, smiting the

Vale of Anduin with hail and lightning, and casting its shadow
upon Minas Tirith with threat of war. Then, lowering in the
mountains, and gathering its great spires, it rolled on slowly
over Gondor and the skirts of Rohan, until far away the
Riders on the plain saw its black towers moving behind the
sun, as they rode into the West. But here, over the desert
and the reeking marshes the deep blue sky of evening opened
once more, and a few pallid stars appeared, like small white
holes in the canopy above the crescent moon.

'It's good to be able to see again,' said Frodo, breathing
deep. 'Do you know, I thought for a bit that I had lost my
sight? From the lightning or something else worse. I could
see nothing, nothing at all, until the grey rope came down.
It seemed to shimmer somehow.'

'It does look sort of silver in the dark,' said Sam. 'Never
noticed it before, though I can't remember as I've ever had
it out since I first stowed it. But if you're so set on climbing,
Mr. Frodo, how are you going to use it? Thirty ells, or say,
about eighteen fathom: that's no more than your guess at the
height of the cliff.'

Frodo thought for a while. 'Make it fast to that stump,
Sam!' he said. 'Then I think you shall have your wish this
time and go first. I'll lower you, and you need do no more
than use your feet and hands to fend yourself off the rock.
Though, if you put your weight on some of the ledges and
give me a rest, it will help. When you're down, I'll follow. I
feel quite myself again now.'

'Very well,' said Sam heavily. 'If it must be, let's get it
over!' He took up the rope and made it fast over the stump
nearest to the brink; then the other end he tied about his own
waist. Reluctantly he turned and prepared to go over the
edge a second time.

It did not, however, turn out half as bad as he had expected.
The rope seemed to give him confidence, though he shut his
eyes more than once when he looked down between his feet.
There was one awkward spot, where there was no ledge and

the wall was sheer and even undercut for a short space; there he slipped and swung out on the silver line. But Frodo lowered him slowly and steadily, and it was over at last. His chief fear had been that the rope-length would give out while he was still high up, but there was still a good bight in Frodo's hands, when Sam came to the bottom and called up: 'I'm down!' His voice came up clearly from below, but Frodo could not see him; his grey elven-cloak had melted into the twilight.

Frodo took rather more time to follow him. He had the rope about his waist and it was fast above, and he had shortened it so that it would pull him up before he reached the ground; still he did not want to risk a fall, and he had not quite Sam's faith in this slender grey line. He found two places, all the same, where he had to trust wholly to it: smooth surfaces where there was no hold even for his strong hobbit fingers and the ledges were far apart. But at last he too was down.

'Well!' he cried. 'We've done it! We've escaped from the Emyn Muil! And now what next, I wonder? Maybe we shall soon be sighing for good hard rock under foot again.'

But Sam did not answer: he was staring back up the cliff. 'Ninnyhammers!' he said. 'Noodles! My beautiful rope! There it is tied to a stump, and we're at the bottom. Just as nice a little stair for that slinking Gollum as we could leave. Better put up a signpost to say which way we've gone! I thought it seemed a bit too easy.'

'If you can think of any way we could have both used the rope and yet brought it down with us, then you can pass on to me ninnyhammer, or any other name your Gaffer gave you,' said Frodo. 'Climb up and untie it and let yourself down, if you want to!'

Sam scratched his head. 'No, I can't think how, begging your pardon,' he said. 'But I don't like leaving it, and that's a fact.' He stroked the rope's end and shook it gently. 'It goes hard parting with anything I brought out of the Elf-country. Made by Galadriel herself, too, maybe. Galadriel,' he murmured, nodding his head mournfully. He looked up and gave one last pull to the rope as if in farewell.

To the complete surprise of both the hobbits it came loose. Sam fell over, and the long grey coils slithered silently down on top of him. Frodo laughed. 'Who tied the rope?' he said. 'A good thing it held as long as it did! To think that I trusted all my weight to your knot!'

Sam did not laugh. 'I may not be much good at climbing, Mr. Frodo,' he said in injured tones, 'but I do know something about rope and about knots. It's in the family, as you might say. Why, my grand-dad, and my uncle Andy after him, him that was the Gaffer's eldest brother, he had a rope-walk over by Tighfield many a year. And I put as fast a hitch over the stump as any one could have done, in the Shire or out of it.'

'Then the rope must have broken – frayed on the rock-edge, I expect,' said Frodo.

'I bet it didn't!' said Sam in an even more injured voice. He stooped and examined the ends. 'Nor it hasn't neither. Not a strand!'

'Then I'm afraid it must have been the knot,' said Frodo.

Sam shook his head and did not answer. He was passing the rope through his fingers thoughtfully. 'Have it your own way, Mr. Frodo,' he said at last, 'but I think the rope came off itself – when I called.' He coiled it up and stowed it lovingly in his pack.

'It certainly came,' said Frodo, 'and that's the chief thing. But now we've got to think of our next move. Night will be on us soon. How beautiful the stars are, and the Moon!'

'They do cheer the heart, don't they?' said Sam looking up. 'Elvish they are, somehow. And the Moon's growing. We haven't seen him for a night or two in this cloudy weather. He's beginning to give quite a light.'

'Yes,' said Frodo; 'but he won't be full for some days. I don't think we'll try the marshes by the light of half a moon.'

*   *   *

Under the first shadows of night they started out on the next stage of their journey. After a while Sam turned and looked back at the way they had come. The mouth of the gully was a black notch in the dim cliff. 'I'm glad we've got the rope,' he said. 'We've set a little puzzle for that footpad, anyhow. He can try his nasty flappy feet on those ledges!'

They picked their steps away from the skirts of the cliff, among a wilderness of boulders and rough stones, wet and slippery with the heavy rain. The ground still fell away sharply. They had not gone very far when they came upon a great fissure that yawned suddenly black before their feet. It was not wide, but it was too wide to jump across in the dim light. They thought they could hear water gurgling in its depths. It curved away on their left northward, back towards the hills, and so barred their road in that direction, at any rate while darkness lasted.

'We had better try a way back southwards along the line of the cliff, I think,' said Sam. 'We might find some nook there, or even a cave or something.'

'I suppose so,' said Frodo. 'I'm tired, and I don't think I can scramble among stones much longer tonight – though I grudge the delay. I wish there was a clear path in front of us: then I'd go on till my legs gave way.'

They did not find the going any easier at the broken feet of the Emyn Muil. Nor did Sam find any nook or hollow to shelter in: only bare stony slopes frowned over by the cliff, which now rose again, higher and more sheer as they went back. In the end, worn out, they just cast themselves on the ground under the lee of a boulder lying not far from the foot of the precipice. There for some time they sat huddled mournfully together in the cold stony night, while sleep crept upon them in spite of all they could do to hold it off. The moon now rode high and clear. Its thin white light lit up the faces of the rocks and drenched the cold frowning walls of the cliff, turning all the wide looming darkness into a chill pale grey scored with black shadows.

'Well!' said Frodo, standing up and drawing his cloak more closely round him. 'You sleep for a bit Sam and take my blanket. I'll walk up and down on sentry for a while.' Suddenly he stiffened, and stooping he gripped Sam by the arm. 'What's that?' he whispered. 'Look over there on the cliff!'

Sam looked and breathed in sharply through his teeth. 'Ssss!' he said. 'That's what it is. It's that Gollum! Snakes and adders! And to think that I thought that we'd puzzle him with our bit of a climb! Look at him! Like a nasty crawling spider on a wall.'

Down the face of a precipice, sheer and almost smooth it seemed in the pale moonlight, a small black shape was moving with its thin limbs splayed out. Maybe its soft clinging hands and toes were finding crevices and holds that no hobbit could ever have seen or used, but it looked as if it was just creeping down on sticky pads, like some large prowling thing of insect-kind. And it was coming down head first, as if it was smelling its way. Now and again it lifted its head slowly, turning it right back on its long skinny neck, and the hobbits caught a glimpse of two small pale gleaming lights, its eyes that blinked at the moon for a moment and then were quickly lidded again.

'Do you think he can see us?' said Sam.

'I don't know,' said Frodo quietly, 'but I think not. It is hard even for friendly eyes to see these elven-cloaks: I cannot see you in the shadow even at a few paces. And I've heard that he doesn't like Sun or Moon.'

'Then why is he coming down just here?' asked Sam.

'Quietly, Sam!' said Frodo. 'He can smell us, perhaps. And he can hear as keen as Elves, I believe. I think he has heard something now: our voices probably. We did a lot of shouting away back there; and we were talking far too loudly until a minute ago.'

'Well, I'm sick of him,' said Sam. 'He's come once too often for me, and I'm going to have a word with him, if I can. I don't suppose we could give him the slip now anyway.'

Drawing his grey hood well over his face, Sam crept stealthily towards the cliff.

'Careful!' whispered Frodo coming behind. 'Don't alarm him! He's much more dangerous than he looks.'

The black crawling shape was now three-quarters of the way down, and perhaps fifty feet or less above the cliff's foot. Crouching stone-still in the shadow of a large boulder the hobbits watched him. He seemed to have come to a difficult passage or to be troubled about something. They could hear him snuffling, and now and again there was a harsh hiss of breath that sounded like a curse. He lifted his head, and they thought they heard him spit. Then he moved on again. Now they could hear his voice creaking and whistling.

'Ach, sss! Cautious, my precious! More haste less speed. We musstn't rissk our neck, musst we, precious? No, precious – *gollum*!' He lifted his head again, blinked at the moon, and quickly shut his eyes. 'We hate it,' he hissed. 'Nassty, nassty shivery light it is – sss – it spies on us, precious – it hurts our eyes.'

He was getting lower now and the hisses became sharper and clearer. 'Where iss it, where iss it: my Precious, my Precious? It's ours, it is, and we wants it. The thieves, the thieves, the filthy little thieves. Where are they with my Precious? Curse them! We hates them.'

'It doesn't sound as if he knew we were here, does it?' whispered Sam. 'And what's his Precious? Does he mean the——'

'Hsh!' breathed Frodo. 'He's getting near now, near enough to hear a whisper.'

Indeed Gollum had suddenly paused again, and his large head on its scrawny neck was lolling from side to side as if he was listening. His pale eyes were half unlidded. Sam restrained himself, though his fingers were twitching. His eyes, filled with anger and disgust, were fixed on the wretched creature as he now began to move again, still whispering and hissing to himself.

At last he was no more than a dozen feet from the ground, right above their heads. From that point there was a sheer drop, for the cliff was slightly undercut, and even Gollum could not find a hold of any kind. He seemed to be trying to twist round, so as to go legs first, when suddenly with a shrill whistling shriek he fell. As he did so, he curled his legs and arms up round him, like a spider whose descending thread is snapped.

Sam was out of his hiding in a flash and crossed the space between him and the cliff-foot in a couple of leaps. Before Gollum could get up, he was on top of him. But he found Gollum more than he bargained for, even taken like that, suddenly, off his guard after a fall. Before Sam could get a hold, long legs and arms were wound round him pinning his arms, and a clinging grip, soft but horribly strong, was squeezing him like slowly tightening cords; clammy fingers were feeling for his throat. Then sharp teeth bit into his shoulder. All he could do was to butt his hard round head sideways into the creature's face. Gollum hissed and spat, but he did not let go.

Things would have gone ill with Sam, if he had been alone. But Frodo sprang up, and drew Sting from its sheath. With his left hand he drew back Gollum's head by his thin lank hair, stretching his long neck, and forcing his pale venomous eyes to stare up at the sky.

'Let go! Gollum,' he said. 'This is Sting. You have seen it before once upon a time. Let go, or you'll feel it this time! I'll cut your throat.'

Gollum collapsed and went as loose as wet string. Sam got up, fingering his shoulder. His eyes smouldered with anger, but he could not avenge himself: his miserable enemy lay grovelling on the stones whimpering.

'Don't hurt us! Don't let them hurt us, precious! They won't hurt us will they, nice little hobbitses? We didn't mean no harm, but they jumps on us like cats on poor mices, they did, precious. And we're so lonely, *gollum*. We'll be nice to them, very nice, if they'll be nice to us, won't we, yes, yess.'

'Well, what's to be done with it?' said Sam. 'Tie it up, so as it can't come sneaking after us no more, I say.'

'But that would kill us, kill us,' whimpered Gollum. 'Cruel little hobbitses. Tie us up in the cold hard lands and leave us, *gollum, gollum.*' Sobs welled up in his gobbling throat.

'No,' said Frodo. 'If we kill him, we must kill him outright. But we can't do that, not as things are. Poor wretch! He has done us no harm.'

'Oh hasn't he!' said Sam rubbing his shoulder. 'Anyway he meant to, *and* he means to, I'll warrant. Throttle us in our sleep, that's his plan.'

'I daresay,' said Frodo. 'But what he means to do is another matter.' He paused for a while in thought. Gollum lay still, but stopped whimpering. Sam stood glowering over him.

It seemed to Frodo then that he heard, quite plainly but far off, voices out of the past:

What a pity Bilbo did not stab the vile creature, when he had a chance!

Pity? It was Pity that stayed his hand. Pity, and Mercy: not to strike without need.

I do not feel any pity for Gollum. He deserves death.

Deserves death! I daresay he does. Many that live deserve death. And some die that deserve life. Can you give that to them? Then be not too eager to deal out death in the name of justice, fearing for your own safety. Even the wise cannot see all ends.

'Very well,' he answered aloud, lowering his sword. 'But still I am afraid. And yet, as you see, I will not touch the creature. For now that I see him, I do pity him.'

Sam stared at his master, who seemed to be speaking to some one who was not there. Gollum lifted his head.

'Yess, wretched we are, precious,' he whined. 'Misery misery! Hobbits won't kill us, nice hobbits.'

'No, we won't,' said Frodo. 'But we won't let you go, either. You're full of wickedness and mischief, Gollum. You will have to come with us, that's all, while we keep an eye

on you. But you must help us, if you can. One good turn
deserves another.'

'Yess, yes indeed,' said Gollum sitting up. 'Nice hobbits!
We will come with them. Find them safe paths in the dark,
yes we will. And where are they going in these cold hard
lands, we wonders, yes we wonders?' He looked up at them,
and a faint light of cunning and eagerness flickered for a
second in his pale blinking eyes.

Sam scowled at him, and sucked his teeth; but he seemed
to sense that there was something odd about his master's
mood and that the matter was beyond argument. All the
same he was amazed at Frodo's reply.

Frodo looked straight into Gollum's eyes which flinched
and twisted away. 'You know that, or you guess well enough,
Sméagol,' he said, quietly and sternly. 'We are going to
Mordor, of course. And you know the way there, I believe.'

'Ach! sss!' said Gollum, covering his ears with his hands,
as if such frankness, and the open speaking of the names,
hurt him. 'We guessed, yes we guessed,' he whispered; 'and
we didn't want them to go, did we? No, precious, not the
nice hobbits. Ashes, ashes, and dust, and thirst there is; and
pits, pits, pits, and Orcs, thousands of Orcses. Nice hobbits
mustn't go to – sss – those places.'

'So you have been there?' Frodo insisted. 'And you're
being drawn back there, aren't you?'

'Yess. Yess. No!' shrieked Gollum. 'Once, by accident it
was, wasn't it, precious? Yes, by accident. But we won't go
back, no, no!' Then suddenly his voice and language
changed, and he sobbed in his throat, and spoke but not to
them. 'Leave me alone, *gollum*! You hurt me. O my poor
hands, *gollum*! I, we, I don't want to come back. I can't find
it. I am tired. I, we can't find it, *gollum, gollum*, no, nowhere.
They're always awake. Dwarves, Men, and Elves, terrible
Elves with bright eyes. I can't find it. Ach!' He got up and
clenched his long hand into a bony fleshless knot, shaking it
towards the East. 'We won't!' he cried. 'Not for you.' Then
he collapsed again. '*Gollum, gollum*,' he whimpered with his

face to the ground. 'Don't look at us! Go away! Go to sleep!'

'He will not go away or go to sleep at your command, Sméagol,' said Frodo. 'But if you really wish to be free of him again, then you must help me. And that I fear means finding us a path towards him. But you need not go all the way, not beyond the gates of his land.'

Gollum sat up again and looked at him under his eyelids. 'He's over there,' he cackled. 'Always there. Orcs will take you all the way. Easy to find Orcs east of the River. Don't ask Sméagol. Poor, poor Sméagol, he went away long ago. They took his Precious, and he's lost now.'

'Perhaps we'll find him again, if you come with us,' said Frodo.

'No, no, never! He's lost his Precious,' said Gollum.

'Get up!' said Frodo.

Gollum stood up and backed away against the cliff.

'Now!' said Frodo. 'Can you find a path easier by day or by night? We're tired; but if you choose the night, we'll start tonight.'

'The big lights hurt our eyes, they do,' Gollum whined. 'Not under the White Face, not yet. It will go behind the hills soon, yess. Rest a bit first, nice hobbits!'

'Then sit down,' said Frodo, 'and don't move!'

The hobbits seated themselves beside him, one on either side, with their backs to the stony wall, resting their legs. There was no need for any arrangement by word: they knew that they must not sleep for a moment. Slowly the moon went by. Shadows fell down from the hills, and all grew dark before them. The stars grew thick and bright in the sky above. No one stirred. Gollum sat with his legs drawn up, knees under chin, flat hands and feet splayed on the ground, his eyes closed; but he seemed tense, as if thinking or listening.

Frodo looked across at Sam. Their eyes met and they understood. They relaxed, leaning their heads back, and shutting their eyes or seeming to. Soon the sound of their soft breathing could be heard. Gollum's hands twitched a little.

Hardly perceptibly his head moved to the left and the right, and first one eye and then the other opened a slit. The hobbits made no sign.

Suddenly, with startling agility and speed, straight off the ground with a jump like a grasshopper or a frog, Gollum bounded forward into the darkness. But that was just what Frodo and Sam had expected. Sam was on him before he had gone two paces after his spring. Frodo coming behind grabbed his leg and threw him.

'Your rope might prove useful again, Sam,' he said.

Sam got out the rope. 'And where were you off to in the cold hard lands, Mr. Gollum?' he growled. 'We wonders, aye, we wonders. To find some of your orc-friends, I warrant. You nasty treacherous creature. It's round your neck this rope ought to go, and a tight noose too.'

Gollum lay quiet and tried no further tricks. He did not answer Sam, but gave him a swift venomous look.

'All we need is something to keep a hold on him,' said Frodo. 'We want him to walk, so it's no good tying his legs – or his arms, he seems to use them nearly as much. Tie one end to his ankle, and keep a grip on the other end.'

He stood over Gollum, while Sam tied the knot. The result surprised them both. Gollum began to scream, a thin, tearing sound, very horrible to hear. He writhed, and tried to get his mouth to his ankle and bite the rope. He kept on screaming.

At last Frodo was convinced that he really was in pain; but it could not be from the knot. He examined it and found that it was not too tight, indeed hardly tight enough. Sam was gentler than his words. 'What's the matter with you?' he said. 'If you will try to run away, you must be tied; but we don't wish to hurt you.'

'It hurts us, it hurts us,' hissed Gollum. 'It freezes, it bites! Elves twisted it, curse them! Nasty cruel hobbits! That's why we tries to escape, of course it is, precious. We guessed they were cruel hobbits. They visits Elves, fierce Elves with bright eyes. Take it off us! It hurts us.'

'No, I will not take it off you,' said Frodo, 'not unless' –
he paused a moment in thought – 'not unless there is any
promise you can make that I can trust.'

'We will swear to do what he wants, yes, yess,' said Gollum,
still twisting and grabbling at his ankle. 'It hurts us.'

'Swear?' said Frodo.

'Sméagol,' said Gollum suddenly and clearly, opening his
eyes wide and staring at Frodo with a strange light. 'Sméagol
will swear on the Precious.'

Frodo drew himself up, and again Sam was startled by his
words and his stern voice. 'On the Precious? How dare you?'
he said. 'Think!

One Ring to rule them all and in the Darkness bind them.

Would you commit your promise to that, Sméagol? It will
hold you. But it is more treacherous than you are. It may
twist your words. Beware!'

Gollum cowered. 'On the Precious, on the Precious!' he
repeated.

'And what would you swear?' asked Frodo.

'To be very very good,' said Gollum. Then crawling to
Frodo's feet he grovelled before him, whispering hoarsely: a
shudder ran over him, as if the words shook his very bones
with fear. 'Sméagol will swear never, never, to let Him have
it. Never! Sméagol will save it. But he must swear on the
Precious.'

'No! not on it,' said Frodo, looking down at him with stern
pity. 'All you wish is to see it and touch it, if you can, though
you know it would drive you mad. Not on it. Swear by it, if
you will. For you know where it is. Yes, you know, Sméagol.
It is before you.'

For a moment it appeared to Sam that his master had
grown and Gollum had shrunk: a tall stern shadow, a mighty
lord who hid his brightness in grey cloud, and at his feet a
little whining dog. Yet the two were in some way akin and
not alien: they could reach one another's minds. Gollum

raised himself and began pawing at Frodo, fawning at his knees.

'Down! down!' said Frodo. 'Now speak your promise!'

'We promises, yes I promise!' said Gollum. 'I will serve the master of the Precious. Good master, good Sméagol, *gollum*, *gollum*!' Suddenly he began to weep and bite at his ankle again.

'Take the rope off, Sam!' said Frodo.

Reluctantly Sam obeyed. At once Gollum got up and began prancing about, like a whipped cur whose master has patted it. From that moment a change, which lasted for some time, came over him. He spoke with less hissing and whining, and he spoke to his companions direct, not to his precious self. He would cringe and flinch, if they stepped near him or made any sudden movement, and he avoided the touch of their elven-cloaks; but he was friendly, and indeed pitifully anxious to please. He would cackle with laughter and caper, if any jest was made, or even if Frodo spoke kindly to him, and weep if Frodo rebuked him. Sam said little to him of any sort. He suspected him more deeply than ever, and if possible liked the new Gollum, the Sméagol, less than the old.

'Well, Gollum, or whatever it is we're to call you,' he said, 'now for it! The Moon's gone, and the night's going. We'd better start.'

'Yes, yes,' agreed Gollum, skipping about. 'Off we go! There's only one way across between the North-end and the South-end. I found it, I did. Orcs don't use it, Orcs don't know it. Orcs don't cross the Marshes, they go round for miles and miles. Very lucky you came this way. Very lucky you found Sméagol, yes. Follow Sméagol!'

He took a few steps away and looked back inquiringly, like a dog inviting them for a walk. 'Wait a bit, Gollum!' cried Sam. 'Not too far ahead now! I'm going to be at your tail, and I've got the rope handy.'

'No, no!' said Gollum. 'Sméagol promised.'

In the deep of night under hard clear stars they set off.

Gollum led them back northward for a while along the way they had come; then he slanted to the right away from the steep edge of the Emyn Muil, down the broken stony slopes towards the vast fens below. They faded swiftly and softly into the darkness. Over all the leagues of waste before the gates of Mordor there was a black silence.

CHAPTER II

THE PASSAGE OF THE MARSHES

Gollum moved quickly, with his head and neck thrust forward, often using his hands as well as his feet. Frodo and Sam were hard put to it to keep up with him; but he seemed no longer to have any thought of escaping, and if they fell behind, he would turn and wait for them. After a time he brought them to the brink of the narrow gully that they had struck before; but they were now further from the hills.

'Here it is!' he cried. 'There is a way down inside, yes. Now we follows it – out, out away over there.' He pointed south and east towards the marshes. The reek of them came to their nostrils, heavy and foul even in the cool night air.

Gollum cast up and down along the brink, and at length he called to them. 'Here! We can get down here. Sméagol went this way once: I went this way, hiding from Orcs.'

He led the way, and following him the hobbits climbed down into the gloom. It was not difficult, for the rift was at this point only some fifteen feet deep and about a dozen across. There was running water at the bottom: it was in fact the bed of one of the many small rivers that trickled down from the hills to feed the stagnant pools and mires beyond. Gollum turned to the right, southward more or less, and splashed along with his feet in the shallow stony stream. He seemed greatly delighted to feel the water, and chuckled to himself, sometimes even croaking in a sort of song.

> *The cold hard lands*
> *they bites our hands,*
> *they gnaws our feet.*

> *The rocks and stones*
> *are like old bones*
>   *all bare of meat.*
> *But stream and pool*
> *is wet and cool:*
>   *so nice for feet!*
> *And now we wish——*

'Ha! ha! What does we wish?' he said, looking sidelong at the hobbits. 'We'll tell you,' he croaked. 'He guessed it long ago, Baggins guessed it.' A glint came into his eyes, and Sam catching the gleam in the darkness thought it far from pleasant.

> *Alive without breath;*
> *as cold as death;*
> *never thirsting, ever drinking;*
> *clad in mail, never clinking.*
> *Drowns on dry land,*
> *thinks an island*
> *is a mountain;*
> *thinks a fountain*
> *is a puff of air.*
> *So sleek, so fair!*
>   *What a joy to meet!*
> *We only wish*
> *to catch a fish,*
>   *so juicy-sweet!*

These words only made more pressing to Sam's mind a problem that had been troubling him from the moment when he understood that his master was going to adopt Gollum as a guide: the problem of food. It did not occur to him that his master might also have thought of it, but he supposed Gollum had. Indeed how had Gollum kept himself in all his lonely wandering? 'Not too well,' thought Sam. 'He looks fair famished. Not too dainty to try what hobbit tastes like, if there ain't no fish, I'll wager – supposing as he could catch us napping. Well, he won't: not Sam Gamgee for one.'

They stumbled along in the dark winding gully for a long time, or so it seemed to the tired feet of Frodo and Sam. The gully turned eastward, and as they went on it broadened and got gradually shallower. At last the sky above grew faint with the first grey of morning. Gollum had shown no signs of tiring, but now he looked up and halted.

'Day is near,' he whispered, as if Day was something that might overhear him and spring on him. 'Sméagol will stay here: I will stay here, and the Yellow Face won't see me.'

'We should be glad to see the Sun,' said Frodo, 'but we will stay here: we are too tired to go any further at present.'

'You are not wise to be glad of the Yellow Face,' said Gollum. 'It shows you up. Nice sensible hobbits stay with Sméagol. Orcs and nasty things are about. They can see a long way. Stay and hide with me!'

The three of them settled down to rest at the foot of the rocky wall of the gully. It was not much more than a tall man's height now, and at its base there were wide flat shelves of dry stone; the water ran in a channel on the other side. Frodo and Sam sat on one of the flats, resting their backs. Gollum paddled and scrabbled in the stream.

'We must take a little food,' said Frodo. 'Are you hungry, Sméagol? We have very little to share, but we will spare you what we can.'

At the word *hungry* a greenish light was kindled in Gollum's pale eyes, and they seemed to protrude further than ever from his thin sickly face. For a moment he relapsed into his old Gollum-manner. 'We are famisshed, yes famisshed we are, precious,' he said. 'What is it they eats? Have they nice fisshes?' His tongue lolled out between his sharp yellow teeth, licking his colourless lips.

'No, we have got no fish,' said Frodo. 'We have only got this' – he held up a wafer of *lembas* – 'and water, if the water here is fit to drink.'

'Yess, yess, nice water,' said Gollum. 'Drink it, drink it, while we can! But what is it they've got, precious? Is it crunchable? Is it tasty?'

Frodo broke off a portion of a wafer and handed it to him on its leaf-wrapping. Gollum sniffed at the leaf and his face changed: a spasm of disgust came over it, and a hint of his old malice. 'Sméagol smells it!' he said. 'Leaves out of the elf-country, gah! They stinks. He climbed in those trees, and he couldn't wash the smell off his hands, my nice hands.' Dropping the leaf, he took a corner of the *lembas* and nibbled it. He spat, and a fit of coughing shook him.

'Ach! No!' he spluttered. 'You try to choke poor Sméagol. Dust and ashes, he can't eat that. He must starve. But Sméagol doesn't mind. Nice hobbits! Sméagol has promised. He will starve. He can't eat hobbits' food. He will starve. Poor thin Sméagol!'

'I'm sorry,' said Frodo; 'but I can't help you, I'm afraid. I think this food would do you good, if you would try. But perhaps you can't even try, not yet anyway.'

The hobbits munched their *lembas* in silence. Sam thought that it tasted far better, somehow, than it had for a good while: Gollum's behaviour had made him attend to its flavour again. But he did not feel comfortable. Gollum watched every morsel from hand to mouth, like an expectant dog by a diner's chair. Only when they had finished and were preparing to rest, was he apparently convinced that they had no hidden dainties that he could share in. Then he went and sat by himself a few paces away and whimpered a little.

'Look here!' Sam whispered to Frodo, not too softly: he did not really care whether Gollum heard him or not. 'We've got to get some sleep; but not both together with that hungry villain nigh, promise or no promise. Sméagol or Gollum, he won't change his habits in a hurry, I'll warrant. You go to sleep, Mr. Frodo, and I'll call you when I can't keep my eyelids propped up. Turn and about, same as before, while he's loose.'

'Perhaps you're right, Sam,' said Frodo speaking openly. 'There *is* a change in him, but just what kind of a change and how deep, I'm not sure yet. Seriously though, I don't think there is any need for fear – at present. Still watch if you wish. Give me about two hours, not more, and then call me.'

So tired was Frodo that his head fell forward on his breast and he slept, almost as soon as he had spoken the words. Gollum seemed no longer to have any fears. He curled up and went quickly to sleep, quite unconcerned. Presently his breath was hissing softly through his clenched teeth, but he lay still as stone. After a while, fearing that he would drop off himself, if he sat listening to his two companions breathing, Sam got up and gently prodded Gollum. His hands uncurled and twitched, but he made no other movement. Sam bent down and said *fissh* close to his ear, but there was no response, not even a catch in Gollum's breathing.

Sam scratched his head. 'Must really be asleep,' he muttered. 'And if I was like Gollum, he wouldn't wake up never again.' He restrained the thoughts of his sword and the rope that sprang to his mind, and went and sat down by his master.

When he woke up the sky above was dim, not lighter but darker than when they had breakfasted. Sam leapt to his feet. Not least from his own feeling of vigour and hunger, he suddenly understood that he had slept the daylight away, nine hours at least. Frodo was still fast asleep, lying now stretched on his side. Gollum was not to be seen. Various reproachful names for himself came to Sam's mind, drawn from the Gaffer's large paternal word-hoard; then it also occurred to him that his master had been right: there had for the present been nothing to guard against. They were at any rate both alive and unthrottled.

'Poor wretch!' he said half remorsefully. 'Now I wonder where he's got to?'

'Not far, not far!' said a voice above him. He looked up and saw the shape of Gollum's large head and ears against the evening sky.

'Here, what are you doing?' cried Sam, his suspicions coming back as soon as he saw that shape.

'Sméagol is hungry,' said Gollum. 'Be back soon.'

'Come back now!' shouted Sam. 'Hi! Come back!' But Gollum had vanished.

Frodo woke at the sound of Sam's shout and sat up, rubbing his eyes. 'Hullo!' he said. 'Anything wrong? What's the time?'

'I dunno,' said Sam. 'After sundown, I reckon. And he's gone off. Says he's hungry.'

'Don't worry!' said Frodo. 'There's no help for it. But he'll come back, you'll see. The promise will hold yet a while. And he won't leave his Precious, anyway.'

Frodo made light of it when he learned that they had slept soundly for hours with Gollum, and a very hungry Gollum too, loose beside them. 'Don't think of any of your Gaffer's hard names,' he said. 'You were worn out, and it has turned out well: we are now both rested. And we have a hard road ahead, the worst road of all.'

'About the food,' said Sam. 'How long's it going to take us to do this job? And when it's done, what are we going to do then? This waybread keeps you on your legs in a wonderful way, though it doesn't satisfy the innards proper, as you might say: not to my feeling anyhow, meaning no disrespect to them as made it. But you have to eat some of it every day, and it doesn't grow. I reckon we've got enough to last, say, three weeks or so, and that with a tight belt and a light tooth, mind you. We've been a bit free with it so far.'

'I don't know how long we shall take to – to finish,' said Frodo. 'We were miserably delayed in the hills. But Samwise Gamgee, my dear hobbit – indeed, Sam my dearest hobbit, friend of friends – I do not think we need give thought to what comes after that. To *do the job* as you put it – what hope is there that we ever shall? And if we do, who knows what will come of that? If the One goes into the Fire, and we are at hand? I ask you, Sam, are we ever likely to need bread again? I think not. If we can nurse our limbs to bring us to Mount Doom, that is all we can do. More than I can, I begin to feel.'

Sam nodded silently. He took his master's hand and bent over it. He did not kiss it, though his tears fell on it. Then he turned away, drew his sleeve over his nose, and got up, and stamped about, trying to whistle, and saying between the efforts: 'Where's that dratted creature?'

It was actually not long before Gollum returned; but he came so quietly that they did not hear him till he stood before them. His fingers and face were soiled with black mud. He was still chewing and slavering. What he was chewing, they did not ask or like to think.

'Worms or beetles or something slimy out of holes,' thought Sam. 'Brr! The nasty creature; the poor wretch!'

Gollum said nothing to them, until he had drunk deeply and washed himself in the stream. Then he came up to them, licking his lips. 'Better now,' he said. 'Are we rested? Ready to go on? Nice hobbits, they sleep beautifully. Trust Sméagol now? Very, very good.'

The next stage of their journey was much the same as the last. As they went on the gully became ever shallower and the slope of its floor more gradual. Its bottom was less stony and more earthy, and slowly its sides dwindled to mere banks. It began to wind and wander. That night drew to its end, but clouds were now over moon and star, and they knew of the coming of day only by the slow spreading of the thin grey light.

In a chill hour they came to the end of the water-course. The banks became moss-grown mounds. Over the last shelf of rotting stone the stream gurgled and fell down into a brown bog and was lost. Dry reeds hissed and rattled though they could feel no wind.

On either side and in front wide fens and mires now lay, stretching away southward and eastward into the dim half-light. Mists curled and smoked from dark and noisome pools.

The reek of them hung stifling in the still air. Far away, now almost due south, the mountain-walls of Mordor loomed, like a black bar of rugged clouds floating above a dangerous fog-bound sea.

The hobbits were now wholly in the hands of Gollum. They did not know, and could not guess in that misty light, that they were in fact only just within the northern borders of the marshes, the main expanse of which lay south of them. They could, if they had known the lands, with some delay have retraced their steps a little, and then turning east have come round over hard roads to the bare plain of Dagorlad: the field of the ancient battle before the gates of Mordor. Not that there was great hope in such a course. On that stony plain there was no cover, and across it ran the highways of the Orcs and the soldiers of the Enemy. Not even the cloaks of Lórien would have concealed them there.

'How do we shape our course now, Sméagol?' asked Frodo. 'Must we cross these evil-smelling fens?'

'No need, no need at all,' said Gollum. 'Not if hobbits want to reach the dark mountains and go to see Him very quick. Back a little, and round a little' – his skinny arm waved north and east – 'and you can come on hard cold roads to the very gates of His country. Lots of His people will be there looking out for guests, very pleased to take them straight to Him, O yes. His Eye watches that way all the time. It caught Sméagol there, long ago.' Gollum shuddered. 'But Sméagol has used his eyes since then, yes, yes: I've used eyes and feet and nose since then. I know other ways. More difficult, not so quick; but better, if we don't want Him to see. Follow Sméagol! He can take you through the marshes, through the mists, nice thick mists. Follow Sméagol very carefully, and you may go a long way, quite a long way, before He catches you, yes perhaps.'

It was already day, a windless and sullen morning, and the marsh-reeks lay in heavy banks. No sun pierced the low clouded sky, and Gollum seemed anxious to continue the journey at once. So after a brief rest they set out again and were soon lost in a shadowy silent world, cut off from all view of the lands about, either the hills that they had left or the mountains that they sought. They went slowly in single file: Gollum, Sam, Frodo.

Frodo seemed the most weary of the three, and slow though they went, he often lagged. The hobbits soon found that what had looked like one vast fen was really an endless network of pools, and soft mires, and winding half-strangled water-courses. Among these a cunning eye and foot could thread a wandering path. Gollum certainly had that cunning, and needed all of it. His head on its long neck was ever turning this way and that, while he sniffed and muttered all the time to himself. Sometimes he would hold up his hand and halt them, while he went forward a little, crouching, testing the ground with fingers or toes, or merely listening with one ear pressed to the earth.

It was dreary and wearisome. Cold clammy winter still held sway in this forsaken country. The only green was the scum of livid weed on the dark greasy surfaces of the sullen waters. Dead grasses and rotting reeds loomed up in the mists like ragged shadows of long-forgotten summers.

As the day wore on the light increased a little, and the mists lifted, growing thinner and more transparent. Far above the rot and vapours of the world the Sun was riding high and golden now in a serene country with floors of dazzling foam, but only a passing ghost of her could they see below, bleared, pale, giving no colour and no warmth. But even at this faint reminder of her presence Gollum scowled and flinched. He halted their journey, and they rested, squatting like little hunted animals, in the borders of a great brown reed-thicket. There was a deep silence, only scraped on its surfaces by the faint quiver of empty seed-plumes, and broken grass-blades trembling in small air-movements that they could not feel.

'Not a bird!' said Sam mournfully.

'No, no birds,' said Gollum. 'Nice birds!' He licked his
teeth. 'No birds here. There are snakeses, wormses, things
in the pools. Lots of things, lots of nasty things. No birds,'
he ended sadly. Sam looked at him with distaste.

So passed the third day of their journey with Gollum.
Before the shadows of evening were long in happier lands,
they went on again, always on and on with only brief halts.
These they made not so much for rest as to help Gollum;
for now even he had to go forward with great care, and he
was sometimes at a loss for a while. They had come to the
very midst of the Dead Marshes, and it was dark.

They walked slowly, stooping, keeping close in line, following attentively every move that Gollum made. The fens grew
more wet, opening into wide stagnant meres, among which
it grew more and more difficult to find the firmer places
where feet could tread without sinking into gurgling mud.
The travellers were light, or maybe none of them would ever
have found a way through.

Presently it grew altogether dark: the air itself seemed black
and heavy to breathe. When lights appeared Sam rubbed his
eyes: he thought his head was going queer. He first saw one
with the corner of his left eye, a wisp of pale sheen that faded
away; but others appeared soon after: some like dimly shining
smoke, some like misty flames flickering slowly above unseen
candles; here and there they twisted like ghostly sheets
unfurled by hidden hands. But neither of his companions
spoke a word.

At last Sam could bear it no longer. 'What's all this, Gollum?' he said in a whisper. 'These lights? They're all round
us now. Are we trapped? Who are they?'

Gollum looked up. A dark water was before him, and he
was crawling on the ground, this way and that, doubtful of
the way. 'Yes, they are all round us,' he whispered. 'The
tricksy lights. Candles of corpses, yes, yes. Don't you heed
them! Don't look! Don't follow them! Where's the master?'

Sam looked back and found that Frodo had lagged again.

He could not see him. He went some paces back into the darkness, not daring to move far, or to call in more than a hoarse whisper. Suddenly he stumbled against Frodo, who was standing lost in thought, looking at the pale lights. His hands hung stiff at his sides; water and slime were dripping from them.

'Come, Mr. Frodo!' said Sam. 'Don't look at them! Gollum says we mustn't. Let's keep up with him and get out of this cursed place as quick as we can – if we can!'

'All right,' said Frodo, as if returning out of a dream. 'I'm coming. Go on!'

Hurrying forward again, Sam tripped, catching his foot in some old root or tussock. He fell and came heavily on his hands, which sank deep into sticky ooze, so that his face was brought close to the surface of the dark mere. There was a faint hiss, a noisome smell went up, the lights flickered and danced and swirled. For a moment the water below him looked like some window, glazed with grimy glass, through which he was peering. Wrenching his hands out of the bog, he sprang back with a cry. 'There are dead things, dead faces in the water,' he said with horror. 'Dead faces!'

Gollum laughed. 'The Dead Marshes, yes, yes: that is their name,' he cackled. 'You should not look in when the candles are lit.'

'Who are they? What are they?' asked Sam shuddering, turning to Frodo, who was now behind him.

'I don't know,' said Frodo in a dreamlike voice. 'But I have seen them too. In the pools when the candles were lit. They lie in all the pools, pale faces, deep deep under the dark water. I saw them: grim faces and evil, and noble faces and sad. Many faces proud and fair, and weeds in their silver hair. But all foul, all rotting, all dead. A fell light is in them.' Frodo hid his eyes in his hands. 'I know not who they are; but I thought I saw there Men and Elves, and Orcs beside them.'

'Yes, yes,' said Gollum. 'All dead, all rotten. Elves and Men and Orcs. The Dead Marshes. There was a great battle

long ago, yes, so they told him when Sméagol was young,
when I was young before the Precious came. It was a great
battle. Tall Men with long swords, and terrible Elves, and
Orcses shrieking. They fought on the plain for days and
months at the Black Gates. But the Marshes have grown
since then, swallowed up the graves; always creeping,
creeping.'

'But that is an age and more ago,' said Sam. 'The Dead
can't be really there! Is it some devilry hatched in the Dark
Land?'

'Who knows? Sméagol doesn't know,' answered Gollum.
'You cannot reach them, you cannot touch them. We tried
once, yes, precious. I tried once; but you cannot reach them.
Only shapes to see, perhaps, not to touch. No precious! All
dead.'

Sam looked darkly at him and shuddered again, thinking
that he guessed why Sméagol had tried to touch them. 'Well,
I don't want to see them,' he said. 'Never again! Can't we
get on and get away?'

'Yes, yes,' said Gollum. 'But slowly, very slowly. Very
carefully! Or hobbits go down to join the Dead ones and
light little candles. Follow Sméagol! Don't look at lights!'

He crawled away to the right, seeking for a path round
the mere. They came close behind, stooping, often using
their hands even as he did. 'Three precious little Gollums in
a row we shall be, if this goes on much longer,' thought
Sam.

At last they came to the end of the black mere, and they
crossed it, perilously, crawling or hopping from one treacherous island tussock to another. Often they floundered, step-
ping or falling hands-first into waters as noisome as a
cesspool, till they were slimed and fouled almost up to their
necks and stank in one another's nostrils.

It was late in the night when at length they reached firmer
ground again. Gollum hissed and whispered to himself, but
it appeared that he was pleased: in some mysterious way, by

some blended sense of feel, and smell, and uncanny memory
for shapes in the dark, he seemed to know just where he was
again, and to be sure of his road ahead.

'Now on we go!' he said. 'Nice hobbits! Brave hobbits!
Very very weary, of course; so we are, my precious, all of
us. But we must take master away from the wicked lights,
yes, yes, we must.' With these words he started off again,
almost at a trot, down what appeared to be a long lane
between high reeds, and they stumbled after him as quickly
as they could. But in a little while he stopped suddenly and
sniffed the air doubtfully, hissing as if he was troubled or
displeased again.

'What is it?' growled Sam, misinterpreting the signs.
'What's the need to sniff? The stink nearly knocks me down
with my nose held. You stink, and master stinks; the whole
place stinks.'

'Yes, yes, and Sam stinks!' answered Gollum. 'Poor Sméa-
gol smells it, but good Sméagol bears it. Helps nice master.
But that's no matter. The air's moving, change is coming.
Sméagol wonders; he's not happy.'

He went on again, but his uneasiness grew, and every now
and again he stood up to his full height, craning his neck
eastward and southward. For some time the hobbits could
not hear or feel what was troubling him. Then suddenly all
three halted, stiffening and listening. To Frodo and Sam it
seemed that they heard, far away, a long wailing cry, high
and thin and cruel. They shivered. At the same moment the
stirring of the air became perceptible to them; and it grew
very cold. As they stood straining their ears, they heard a
noise like a wind coming in the distance. The misty lights
wavered, dimmed, and went out.

Gollum would not move. He stood shaking and gibbering
to himself, until with a rush the wind came upon them, hissing
and snarling over the marshes. The night became less dark,
light enough for them to see, or half see, shapeless drifts of
fog, curling and twisting as it rolled over them and passed

them. Looking up they saw the clouds breaking and shred-
ding; and then high in the south the moon glimmered out,
riding in the flying wrack.

For a moment the sight of it gladdened the hearts of the
hobbits; but Gollum cowered down, muttering curses on the
White Face. Then Frodo and Sam staring at the sky, breathing deeply of the fresher air, saw it come: a small cloud flying
from the accursed hills; a black shadow loosed from Mordor;
a vast shape winged and ominous. It scudded across the
moon, and with a deadly cry went away westward, out-
running the wind in its fell speed.

They fell forward, grovelling heedlessly on the cold earth.
But the shadow of horror wheeled and returned, passing
lower now, right above them, sweeping the fen-reek with its
ghastly wings. And then it was gone, flying back to Mordor
with the speed of the wrath of Sauron; and behind it the
wind roared away, leaving the Dead Marshes bare and bleak.
The naked waste, as far as the eye could pierce, even to the
distant menace of the mountains, was dappled with the fitful
moonlight.

Frodo and Sam got up, rubbing their eyes, like children
wakened from an evil dream to find the familiar night still
over the world. But Gollum lay on the ground as if he had
been stunned. They roused him with difficulty, and for some
time he would not lift his face, but knelt forward on his
elbows, covering the back of his head with his large flat
hands.

'Wraiths!' he wailed. 'Wraiths on wings! The Precious is
their master. They see everything, everything. Nothing can
hide from them. Curse the White Face! And they tell Him
everything. He sees, He knows. Ach, *gollum, gollum, gollum*!'
It was not until the moon had sunk, westering far away
beyond Tol Brandir, that he would get up or make a move.

From that time on Sam thought that he sensed a change
in Gollum again. He was more fawning and would-be
friendly; but Sam surprised some strange looks in his eyes

at times, especially towards Frodo; and he went back more and more into his old manner of speaking. And Sam had another growing anxiety. Frodo seemed to be weary, weary to the point of exhaustion. He said nothing, indeed he hardly spoke at all; and he did not complain, but he walked like one who carries a load, the weight of which is ever increasing; and he dragged along, slower and slower, so that Sam had often to beg Gollum to wait and not to leave their master behind.

In fact with every step towards the gates of Mordor Frodo felt the Ring on its chain about his neck grow more burden-some. He was now beginning to feel it as an actual weight dragging him earthwards. But far more he was troubled by the Eye: so he called it to himself. It was that more than the drag of the Ring that made him cower and stoop as he walked. The Eye: that horrible growing sense of a hostile will that strove with great power to pierce all shadows of cloud, and earth, and flesh, and to see you: to pin you under its deadly gaze, naked, immovable. So thin, so frail and thin, the veils were become that still warded it off. Frodo knew just where the present habitation and heart of that will now was: as certainly as a man can tell the direction of the sun with his eyes shut. He was facing it, and its potency beat upon his brow.

Gollum probably felt something of the same sort. But what went on in his wretched heart between the pressure of the Eye, and the lust of the Ring that was so near, and his grovel-ling promise made half in the fear of cold iron, the hobbits did not guess. Frodo gave no thought to it. Sam's mind was occupied mostly with his master, hardly noticing the dark cloud that had fallen on his own heart. He put Frodo in front of him now, and kept a watchful eye on every movement of his, supporting him if he stumbled, and trying to encourage him with clumsy words.

When day came at last the hobbits were surprised to see how much closer the ominous mountains had already drawn.

The air was now clearer and colder, and though still far off, the walls of Mordor were no longer a cloudy menace on the edge of sight, but as grim black towers they frowned across a dismal waste. The marshes were at an end, dying away into dead peats and wide flats of dry cracked mud. The land ahead rose in long shallow slopes, barren and pitiless, towards the desert that lay at Sauron's gate.

While the grey light lasted, they cowered under a black stone like worms, shrinking, lest the winged terror should pass and spy them with its cruel eyes. The remainder of that journey was a shadow of growing fear in which memory could find nothing to rest upon. For two more nights they struggled on through the weary pathless land. The air, as it seemed to them, grew harsh, and filled with a bitter reek that caught their breath and parched their mouths.

At last, on the fifth morning since they took the road with Gollum, they halted once more. Before them dark in the dawn the great mountains reached up to roofs of smoke and cloud. Out from their feet were flung huge buttresses and broken hills that were now at the nearest scarce a dozen miles away. Frodo looked round in horror. Dreadful as the Dead Marshes had been, and the arid moors of the Noman-lands, more loathsome far was the country that the crawling day now slowly unveiled to his shrinking eyes. Even to the Mere of Dead Faces some haggard phantom of green spring would come; but here neither spring nor summer would ever come again. Here nothing lived, not even the leprous growths that feed on rottenness. The gasping pools were choked with ash and crawling muds, sickly white and grey, as if the mountains had vomited the filth of their entrails upon the lands about. High mounds of crushed and powdered rock, great cones of earth fire-blasted and poison-stained, stood like an obscene graveyard in endless rows, slowly revealed in the reluctant light.

They had come to the desolation that lay before Mordor: the lasting monument to the dark labour of its slaves that should endure when all their purposes were made void; a

land defiled, diseased beyond all healing – unless the Great
Sea should enter in and wash it with oblivion. 'I feel sick,'
said Sam. Frodo did not speak.

For a while they stood there, like men on the edge of a
sleep where nightmare lurks, holding it off, though they know
that they can only come to morning through the shadows.
The light broadened and hardened. The gasping pits and
poisonous mounds grew hideously clear. The sun was up,
walking among clouds and long flags of smoke, but even the
sunlight was defiled. The hobbits had no welcome for that
light; unfriendly it seemed, revealing them in their helpless-
ness – little squeaking ghosts that wandered among the ash-
heaps of the Dark Lord.

Too weary to go further they sought for some place
where they could rest. For a while they sat without speaking
under the shadow of a mound of slag; but foul fumes
leaked out of it, catching their throats and choking them.
Gollum was the first to get up. Spluttering and cursing he
rose, and without a word or a glance at the hobbits he crawled
away on all fours. Frodo and Sam crawled after him until
they came to a wide almost circular pit, high-banked upon
the west. It was cold and dead, and a foul sump of oily
many-coloured ooze lay at its bottom. In this evil hole they
cowered, hoping in its shadow to escape the attention of
the Eye.

The day passed slowly. A great thirst troubled them, but
they drank only a few drops from their bottles – last filled in
the gully, which now as they looked back in thought seemed
to them a place of peace and beauty. The hobbits took it in
turn to watch. At first, tired as they were, neither of them
could sleep at all; but as the sun far away was climbing down
into slow moving cloud, Sam dozed. It was Frodo's turn to
be on guard. He lay back on the slope of the pit, but that
did not ease the sense of burden that was on him. He looked
up at the smoke-streaked sky and saw strange phantoms,
dark riding shapes, and faces out of the past. He lost count of

time, hovering between sleep and waking, until forgetfulness came over him.

Suddenly Sam woke up thinking that he heard his master calling. It was evening. Frodo could not have called, for he had fallen asleep, and had slid down nearly to the bottom of the pit. Gollum was by him. For a moment Sam thought that he was trying to rouse Frodo; then he saw that it was not so. Gollum was talking to himself. Sméagol was holding a debate with some other thought that used the same voice but made it squeak and hiss. A pale light and a green light alternated in his eyes as he spoke.

'Sméagol promised,' said the first thought.

'Yes, yes, my precious,' came the answer, 'we promised: to save our Precious, not to let Him have it – never. But it's going to Him, yes, nearer every step. What's the hobbit going to do with it, we wonders, yes we wonders.'

'I don't know. I can't help it. Master's got it. Sméagol promised to help the master.'

'Yes, yes, to help the master: the master of the Precious. But if we was master, then we could help ourselfs, yes, and still keep promises.'

'But Sméagol said he would be very very good. Nice hobbit! He took cruel rope off Sméagol's leg. He speaks nicely to me.'

'Very very good, eh, my precious? Let's be good, good as fish, sweet one, but to ourselfs. Not hurt the nice hobbit, of course, no, no.'

'But the Precious holds the promise,' the voice of Sméagol objected.

'Then take it,' said the other, 'and let's hold it ourselfs! Then we shall be master, *gollum*! Make the other hobbit, the nasty suspicious hobbit, make him crawl, yes, *gollum*!'

'But not the nice hobbit?'

'Oh no, not if it doesn't please us. Still he's a Baggins, my precious, yes, a Baggins. A Baggins stole it. He found it and he said nothing, nothing. We hates Bagginses.'

'No, not this Baggins.'

'Yes, every Baggins. All peoples that keep the Precious. We must have it!'

'But He'll see, He'll know. He'll take it from us!'

'He sees. He knows. He heard us make silly promises – against His orders, yes. Must take it. The Wraiths are searching. Must take it.'

'Not for Him!'

'No, sweet one. See, my precious: if we has it, then we can escape, even from Him, eh? Perhaps we grows very strong, stronger than Wraiths. Lord Sméagol? Gollum the Great? *The* Gollum! Eat fish every day, three times a day, fresh from the sea. Most Precious Gollum! Must have it. We wants it, we wants it, we wants it!'

'But there's two of them. They'll wake too quick and kill us,' whined Sméagol in a last effort. 'Not now. Not yet.'

'We wants it! But' – and here there was a long pause, as if a new thought had wakened. 'Not yet, eh? Perhaps not. She might help. She might, yes.'

'No, no! Not that way!' wailed Sméagol.

'Yes! We wants it! We wants it!'

Each time that the second thought spoke, Gollum's long hand crept out slowly, pawing towards Frodo, and then was drawn back with a jerk as Sméagol spoke again. Finally both arms, with long fingers flexed and twitching, clawed towards his neck.

Sam had lain still, fascinated by this debate, but watching every move that Gollum made from under his half-closed eye-lids. To his simple mind ordinary hunger, the desire to eat hobbits, had seemed the chief danger in Gollum. He realized now that it was not so: Gollum was feeling the terrible call of the Ring. The Dark Lord was *He*, of course; but Sam wondered who *She* was. One of the nasty friends the little wretch had made in his wanderings, he supposed. Then he forgot the point, for things had plainly gone far enough, and were getting dangerous. A great heaviness was in all his limbs, but he roused himself with an effort and sat up. Something warned him to be careful and not to reveal that he had over-heard the debate. He let out a loud sigh and gave a huge yawn.

'What's the time?' he said sleepily.

Gollum sent out a long hiss through his teeth. He stood up for a moment, tense and menacing; and then he collapsed, falling forward on to all fours and crawling up the bank of the pit. 'Nice hobbits! Nice Sam!' he said. 'Sleepy heads, yes, sleepy heads! Leave good Sméagol to watch! But it's evening. Dusk is creeping. Time to go.'

'High time!' thought Sam. 'And time we parted, too.' Yet it crossed his mind to wonder if indeed Gollum was not now as dangerous turned loose as kept with them. 'Curse him! I wish he was choked!' he muttered. He stumbled down the bank and roused his master.

Strangely enough, Frodo felt refreshed. He had been dreaming. The dark shadow had passed, and a fair vision had visited him in this land of disease. Nothing remained of it in his memory, yet because of it he felt glad and lighter of heart. His burden was less heavy on him. Gollum welcomed him with dog-like delight. He chuckled and chattered, crack-ing his long fingers, and pawing at Frodo's knees. Frodo smiled at him.

'Come!' he said. 'You have guided us well and faithfully. This is the last stage. Bring us to the Gate, and then I will not ask you to go further. Bring us to the Gate, and you may go where you wish – only not to our enemies.'

'To the Gate, eh?' Gollum squeaked, seeming surprised and frightened. 'To the Gate, master says! Yes, he says so. And good Sméagol does what he asks, O yes. But when we gets closer, we'll see perhaps, we'll see then. It won't look nice at all. O no! O no!'

'Go on with you!' said Sam. 'Let's get it over!'

In the falling dusk they scrambled out of the pit and slowly threaded their way through the dead land. They had not gone far before they felt once more the fear that had fallen on them when the winged shape swept over the marshes. They halted, cowering on the evil-smelling ground; but they saw nothing in the gloomy evening sky above, and soon the menace passed, high overhead, going maybe on some swift errand from Barad-dûr. After a while Gollum got up and crept forward again, muttering and shaking.

About an hour after midnight the fear fell on them a third time, but it now seemed more remote, as if it were passing far above the clouds, rushing with terrible speed into the West. Gollum, however, was helpless with terror, and was convinced that they were being hunted, that their approach was known.

'Three times!' he whimpered. 'Three times is a threat. They feel us here, they feel the Precious. The Precious is their master. We cannot go any further this way, no. It's no use, no use!'

Pleading and kind words were no longer of any avail. It was not until Frodo commanded him angrily and laid a hand on his sword-hilt that Gollum would get up again. Then at last he rose with a snarl, and went before them like a beaten dog.

So they stumbled on through the weary end of the night, and until the coming of another day of fear they walked in silence with bowed heads, seeing nothing, and hearing nothing but the wind hissing in their ears.

CHAPTER III

THE BLACK GATE IS CLOSED

Before the next day dawned their journey to Mordor was over. The marshes and the desert were behind them. Before them, darkling against a pallid sky, the great mountains reared their threatening heads.

Upon the west of Mordor marched the gloomy range of Ephel Dúath, the Mountains of Shadow, and upon the north the broken peaks and barren ridges of Ered Lithui, grey as ash. But as these ranges approached one another, being indeed but parts of one great wall about the mournful plains of Lithlad and of Gorgoroth, and the bitter inland sea of Núrnen amidmost, they swung out long arms northward; and between these arms there was a deep defile. This was Cirith Gorgor, the Haunted Pass, the entrance to the land of the Enemy. High cliffs lowered upon either side, and thrust forward from its mouth were two sheer hills, black-boned and bare. Upon them stood the Teeth of Mordor, two towers strong and tall. In days long past they were built by the Men of Gondor in their pride and power, after the overthrow of Sauron and his flight, lest he should seek to return to his old realm. But the strength of Gondor failed, and men slept, and for long years the towers stood empty. Then Sauron returned. Now the watch-towers, which had fallen into decay, were repaired, and filled with arms, and garrisoned with ceaseless vigilance. Stony-faced they were, with dark window-holes staring north and east and west, and each window was full of sleepless eyes.

Across the mouth of the pass, from cliff to cliff, the Dark Lord had built a rampart of stone. In it there was a single gate of iron, and upon its battlement sentinels paced unceasingly. Beneath the hills on either side the rock was bored into a hundred caves and maggot-holes; there a host of orcs lurked, ready at a signal to issue forth like black ants going to war. None could pass the Teeth of Mordor and not feel their bite, unless they were summoned by Sauron, or knew the secret passwords that would open the Morannon, the black gate of his land.

The two hobbits gazed at the towers and the wall in despair. Even from a distance they could see in the dim light the movement of the black guards upon the wall, and the patrols before the gate. They lay now peering over the edge of a rocky hollow beneath the outstretched shadow of the northmost buttress of Ephel Dúath. Winging the heavy air in a straight flight a crow, maybe, would have flown but a furlong from their hiding-place to the black summit of the nearer tower. A faint smoke curled above it, as if fire smouldered in the hill beneath.

Day came, and the fallow sun blinked over the lifeless ridges of Ered Lithui. Then suddenly the cry of brazen-throated trumpets was heard: from the watch-towers they blared, and far away from hidden holds and outposts in the hills came answering calls; and further still, remote but deep and ominous, there echoed in the hollow land beyond the mighty horns and drums of Barad-dûr. Another dreadful day of fear and toil had come to Mordor; and the night-guards were summoned to their dungeons and deep halls, and the day-guards, evil-eyed and fell, were marching to their posts. Steel gleamed dimly on the battlement.

'Well, here we are!' said Sam. 'Here's the Gate, and it looks to me as if that's about as far as we are ever going to get. My word, but the Gaffer would have a thing or two to say, if he saw me now! Often said I'd come to a bad end, if I didn't watch my step, he did. But now I don't suppose I'll ever see the old fellow again. He'll miss his chance of *I told 'ee so, Sam*: more's the pity. He could go on telling me as long as he'd got breath, if only I could see his old face again.

But I'd have to get a wash first, or he wouldn't know me.'

'I suppose it's no good asking "what way do we go now?" We can't go no further – unless we want to ask the Orcs for a lift.'

'No, no!' said Gollum. 'No use. We can't go further. Sméagol said so. He said: we'll go to the Gate, and then we'll see. And we do see. O yes, my precious, we do see. Sméagol knew hobbits could not go this way. O yes, Sméagol knew.'

'Then what the plague did you bring us here for?' said Sam, not feeling in the mood to be just or reasonable.

'Master said so. Master says: Bring us to the Gate. So good Sméagol does so. Master said so, wise master.'

'I did,' said Frodo. His face was grim and set, but resolute. He was filthy, haggard, and pinched with weariness, but he cowered no longer, and his eyes were clear. 'I said so, because I purpose to enter Mordor, and I know no other way. Therefore I shall go this way. I do not ask anyone to go with me.'

'No, no, master!' wailed Gollum, pawing at him, and seeming in great distress. 'No use that way! No use! Don't take the Precious to Him! He'll eat us all, if He gets it, eat all the world. Keep it, nice master, and be kind to Sméagol. Don't let Him have it. Or go away, go to nice places, and give it back to little Sméagol. Yes, yes, master give it back, eh? Sméagol will keep it safe; he will do lots of good, especially to nice hobbits. Hobbits go home. Don't go to the Gate!'

'I am commanded to go to the land of Mordor, and therefore I shall go,' said Frodo. 'If there is only one way, then I must take it. What comes after must come.'

Sam said nothing. The look on Frodo's face was enough for him; he knew that words of his were useless. And after all he never had any real hope in the affair from the beginning; but being a cheerful hobbit he had not needed hope, as long as despair could be postponed. Now they were come to the bitter end. But he had stuck to his master all the way; that was what he had chiefly come for, and he would still stick

to him. His master would not go to Mordor alone. Sam
would go with him – and at any rate they would get rid of
Gollum.

Gollum, however, did not intend to be got rid of, yet. He
knelt at Frodo's feet, wringing his hands and squeaking. 'Not
this way, master!' he pleaded. 'There is another way. O yes
indeed there is. Another way, darker, more difficult to find,
more secret. But Sméagol knows it. Let Sméagol show you!'

'Another way!' said Frodo doubtfully, looking down at
Gollum with searching eyes.

'Yess! Yess indeed! There *was* another way. Sméagol found
it. Let's go and see if it's still there!'

'You have not spoken of this before.'

'No. Master did not ask. Master did not say what he meant
to do. He does not tell poor Sméagol. He says: Sméagol, take
me to the Gate – and then good-bye! Sméagol can run away
and be good. But now he says: I purpose to enter Mordor
this way. So Sméagol is very afraid. He does not want to lose
nice master. And he promised, master made him promise,
to save the Precious. But master is going to take it to Him,
straight to the Black Hand, if master will go this way. So
Sméagol must save them both, and he thinks of another way
that there was, once upon a time. Nice master. Sméagol very
good, always helps.'

Sam frowned. If he could have bored holes in Gollum with
his eyes, he would have done. His mind was full of doubt.
To all appearances Gollum was genuinely distressed and
anxious to help Frodo. But Sam, remembering the overheard
debate, found it hard to believe that the long submerged
Sméagol had come out on top: that voice at any rate had not
had the last word in the debate. Sam's guess was that the
Sméagol and Gollum halves (or what in his own mind he
called Slinker and Stinker) had made a truce and a temporary
alliance: neither wanted the Enemy to get the Ring; both
wished to keep Frodo from capture, and under their eye, as
long as possible – at any rate as long as Stinker still had a

chance of laying hands on his 'Precious'. Whether there really was another way into Mordor Sam doubted.

'And it's a good thing neither half of the old villain don't know what master means to do,' he thought. 'If he knew that Mr. Frodo is trying to put an end to his Precious for good and all, there'd be trouble pretty quick, I bet. Anyhow old Stinker is so frightened of the Enemy – and he's under orders of some kind from him, or was – that he'd give us away rather than be caught helping us; and rather than let his Precious be melted, maybe. At least that's my idea. And I hope the master will think it out carefully. He's as wise as any, but he's soft-hearted, that's what he is. It's beyond any Gamgee to guess what he'll do next.'

Frodo did not answer Gollum at once. While these doubts were passing through Sam's slow but shrewd mind, he stood gazing out towards the dark cliff of Cirith Gorgor. The hollow in which they had taken refuge was delved in the side of a low hill, at some little height above a long trenchlike valley that lay between it and the outer buttresses of the mountain-wall. In the midst of the valley stood the black foundations of the western watch-tower. By morning-light the roads that converged upon the Gate of Mordor could now be clearly seen, pale and dusty; one winding back northwards; another dwindling eastwards into the mists that clung about the feet of Ered Lithui; and a third that ran towards him. As it bent sharply round the tower, it entered a narrow defile and passed not far below the hollow where he stood. Westward, to his right, it turned, skirting the shoulders of the mountains, and went off southwards into the deep shadows that mantled all the western sides of Ephel Dúath; beyond his sight it journeyed on into the narrow land between the mountains and the Great River.

As he gazed Frodo became aware that there was a great stir and movement on the plain. It seemed as if whole armies were on the march, though for the most part they were hidden by the reeks and fumes drifting from the fens and wastes beyond. But here and there he caught the gleam of spears and helmets; and over the levels beside the roads horsemen could be seen riding in many companies. He remembered his vision from afar upon Amon Hen, so few days before, though now it seemed many years ago. Then he knew that the hope that had for one wild moment stirred in his heart was vain. The trumpets had not rung in challenge but in greeting. This was no assault upon the Dark Lord by the men of Gondor, risen like avenging ghosts from the graves of valour long passed away. These were Men of other race, out of the wide Eastlands, gathering to the summons of their Overlord; armies that had encamped before his Gate by night and now marched in to swell his mounting power. As if suddenly made fully aware of the peril of their position, alone, in the growing light of day, so near to this vast menace, Frodo quickly drew his frail grey hood close upon his head, and stepped down into the dell. Then he turned to Gollum.

'Sméagol,' he said, 'I will trust you once more. Indeed it seems that I must do so, and that it is my fate to receive help from you, where I least looked for it, and your fate to help me whom you long pursued with evil purpose. So far you have deserved well of me and have kept your promise truly. Truly, I say and mean,' he added with a glance at Sam, 'for twice now we have been in your power, and you have done no harm to us. Nor have you tried to take from me what you once sought. May the third time prove the best! But I warn you, Sméagol, you are in danger.'

'Yes, yes, master!' said Gollum. 'Dreadful danger! Sméagol's bones shake to think of it, but he doesn't run away. He must help nice master.'

'I did not mean the danger that we all share,' said Frodo. 'I mean a danger to yourself alone. You swore a promise by what you call the Precious. Remember that! It will hold you to it; but it will seek a way to twist it to your own undoing. Already you are being twisted. You revealed yourself to me just now, foolishly. *Give it back to Sméagol* you said. Do not say that again! Do not let that thought grow in you! You will never get it back. But the desire of it may betray you to a bitter end. You will never get it back. In the last need, Sméagol, I should put on the Precious; and the Precious mastered you long ago. If I, wearing it, were to command you, you would obey, even if it were to leap from a precipice or to cast yourself into the fire. And such would be my command. So have a care, Sméagol!'

Sam looked at his master with approval, but also with surprise: there was a look in his face and a tone in his voice that he had not known before. It had always been a notion of his that the kindness of dear Mr. Frodo was of such a high degree that it must imply a fair measure of blindness. Of course, he also firmly held the incompatible belief that Mr. Frodo was the wisest person in the world (with the possible exception of Old Mr. Bilbo and of Gandalf). Gollum in his own way, and with much more excuse as his acquaintance was much briefer, may have made a similar mistake, confusing kindness and blindness. At any rate this speech abashed and terrified him. He grovelled on the ground and could speak no clear words but *nice master*.

Frodo waited patiently for a while, then he spoke again less sternly. 'Come now, Gollum or Sméagol if you wish, tell me of this other way, and show me, if you can, what hope there is in it, enough to justify me in turning aside from my plain path. I am in haste.'

But Gollum was in a pitiable state, and Frodo's threat had quite unnerved him. It was not easy to get any clear account out of him, amid his mumblings and squeakings, and the frequent interruptions in which he crawled on the floor and begged them both to be kind to 'poor little Sméagol'. After a while he grew a little calmer, and Frodo gathered bit by bit that, if a traveller followed the road that turned west of Ephel Dúath, he would come in time to a crossing in a circle of dark trees. On the right a road went down to Osgiliath and the bridges of the Anduin; in the middle the road went on southwards.

'On, on, on,' said Gollum. 'We never went that way, but they say it goes a hundred leagues, until you can see the

Great Water that is never still. There are lots of fishes there, and big birds eat fishes: nice birds: but we never went there, alas no! we never had a chance. And further still there are more lands, they say, but the Yellow Face is very hot there, and there are seldom any clouds, and the men are fierce and have dark faces. We do not want to see that land.'

'No!' said Frodo. 'But do not wander from your road. What of the third turning?'

'O yes, O yes, there is a third way,' said Gollum. 'That is the road to the left. At once it begins to climb up, up, winding and climbing back towards the tall shadows. When it turns round the black rock, you'll see it, suddenly you'll see it above you, and you'll want to hide.'

'See it, see it? What will you see?'

'The old fortress, very old, very horrible now. We used to hear tales from the South, when Sméagol was young, long ago. O yes, we used to tell lots of tales in the evening, sitting by the banks of the Great River, in the willow-lands, when the River was younger too, *gollum, gollum.*' He began to weep and mutter. The hobbits waited patiently.

'Tales out of the South,' Gollum went on again, 'about the tall Men with the shining eyes, and their houses like hills of stone, and the silver crown of their King and his White Tree: wonderful tales. They built very tall towers, and one they raised was silver-white, and in it there was a stone like the Moon, and round it were great white walls. O yes, there were many tales about the Tower of the Moon.'

'That would be Minas Ithil that Isildur the son of Elendil built,' said Frodo. 'It was Isildur who cut off the finger of the Enemy.'

'Yes, He has only four on the Black Hand, but they are enough,' said Gollum shuddering. 'And He hated Isildur's city.'

'What does he not hate?' said Frodo. 'But what has the Tower of the Moon to do with us?'

'Well, master, there it was and there it is: the tall tower and the white houses and the wall; but not nice now, not beautiful. He conquered it long ago. It is a very terrible place now. Travellers shiver when they see it, they creep out of sight, they avoid its shadow. But master will have to go that way. That is the only other way. For the mountains are lower there, and the old road goes up and up, until it reaches a dark pass at the top, and then it goes down, down, again – to Gorgoroth.' His voice sank to a whisper and he shuddered.

'But how will that help us?' asked Sam. 'Surely the Enemy knows all about his own mountains, and that road will be guarded as close as this? The tower isn't empty, is it?'

'O no, not empty!' whispered Gollum. 'It seems empty, but it isn't, O no! Very dreadful things live there. Orcs, yes always Orcs; but worse things, worse things live there too. The road climbs right under the shadow of the walls and passes the gate. Nothing moves on the road that they don't know about. The things inside know: the Silent Watchers.'

'So that's your advice is it,' said Sam, 'that we should go another long march south, to find ourselves in the same fix or a worse one, when we get there, if we ever do?'

'No, no indeed,' said Gollum. 'Hobbits must see, must try to understand. He does not expect attack that way. His Eye is all round, but it attends more to some places than to others. He can't see everything all at once, not yet. You see, He has conquered all the country west of the Shadowy Mountains down to the River, and He holds the bridges now. He thinks no one can come to the Moontower without fighting big battle at the bridges, or getting lots of boats which they cannot hide and He will know about.'

'You seem to know a lot about what He's doing and thinking,' said Sam. 'Have you been talking to Him lately? Or just hobnobbing with Orcs?'

'Not nice hobbit, not sensible,' said Gollum, giving Sam an angry glance and turning to Frodo. 'Sméagol has talked to Orcs, yes of course, before he met master, and to many peoples: he has walked very far. And what he says now many peoples are saying. It's here in the North that the big danger is for Him, and for us. He will come out of the Black Gate one day, one day soon. That is the only way big armies can come. But away down west He is not afraid, and there are the Silent Watchers.'

'Just so!' said Sam, not to be put off. 'And so we are to walk up and knock at their gate and ask if we're on the right road for Mordor? Or are they too silent to answer? It's not sense. We might as well do it here, and save ourselves a long tramp.'

'Don't make jokes about it,' hissed Gollum. 'It isn't funny, O no! Not amusing. It's not sense to try and get into Mordor at all. But if master says *I must go* or *I will go*, then he must try some way. But he must not go to the terrible city, O no, of course not. That is where Sméagol helps, nice Sméagol, though no one tells him what it is all about. Sméagol helps again. He found it. He knows it.'

'What did you find?' asked Frodo.

Gollum crouched down and his voice sank to a whisper again. 'A little path leading up into the mountains; and then a stair, a narrow stair, O yes, very long and narrow. And then more stairs. And then' – his voice sank even lower – 'a tunnel, a dark tunnel; and at last a little cleft, and a path high above the main pass. It was that way that Sméagol got out of the darkness. But it was years ago. The path may have vanished now; but perhaps not, perhaps not.'

'I don't like the sound of it at all,' said Sam. 'Sounds too easy at any rate in the telling. If that path is still there, it'll be guarded too. Wasn't it guarded, Gollum?' As he said this, he caught or fancied he caught a green gleam in Gollum's eye. Gollum muttered but did not reply.

'Is it not guarded?' asked Frodo sternly. 'And did you *escape* out of the darkness, Sméagol? Were you not rather permitted to depart, upon an errand? That at least is what Aragorn thought, who found you by the Dead Marshes some years ago.'

'It's a lie!' hissed Gollum, and an evil light came into his eyes at the naming of Aragorn. 'He lied on me, yes he did. I did escape, all by my poor self. Indeed I was told to seek for the Precious; and I have searched and searched, of course I have. But not for the Black One. The Precious was ours, it was mine I tell you. I did escape.'

Frodo felt a strange certainty that in this matter Gollum was for once not so far from the truth as might be suspected; that he had somehow found a way out of Mordor, and at least believed that it was by his own cunning. For one thing, he noted that Gollum used *I*, and that seemed usually to be a sign, on its rare appearances, that some remnants of old truth and sincerity were for the moment on top. But even if Gollum could be trusted on this point, Frodo did not forget the wiles of the Enemy. The 'escape' may have been allowed or arranged, and well known in the Dark Tower. And in any case Gollum was plainly keeping a good deal back.

'I ask you again,' he said: 'is not this secret way guarded?'

But the name of Aragorn had put Gollum into a sullen mood. He had all the injured air of a liar suspected when for once he has told the truth, or part of it. He did not answer.

'Is it not guarded?' Frodo repeated.

'Yes, yes, perhaps. No safe places in this country,' said Gollum sulkily. 'No safe places. But master must try it or go home. No other way.' They could not get him to say more. The name of the perilous place and the high pass he could not tell, or would not.

Its name was Cirith Ungol, a name of dreadful rumour. Aragorn could perhaps have told them that name and its significance; Gandalf would have warned them. But they were alone, and Aragorn was far away, and Gandalf stood amid the ruin of Isengard and strove with Saruman, delayed by treason. Yet even as he spoke his last words to Saruman, and the *palantír* crashed in fire upon the steps of Orthanc, his thought was ever upon Frodo and Samwise, over the long leagues his mind sought for them in hope and pity.

Maybe Frodo felt it, not knowing it, as he had upon Amon Hen, even though he believed that Gandalf was gone, gone for ever into the shadow in Moria far away. He sat upon the ground for a long while, silent, his head bowed, striving to recall all that Gandalf had said to him. But for this choice he could recall no counsel. Indeed Gandalf's guidance had been taken from them too soon, too soon, while the Dark Land was still very far away. How they should enter it at the last Gandalf had not said. Perhaps he could not say. Into the stronghold of the Enemy in the North, into Dol Guldur, he had once ventured. But into Mordor, to the Mountain of Fire and to Barad-dûr, since the Dark Lord rose in power again, had he ever journeyed there? Frodo did not think so. And here he was a little halfling from the Shire, a simple hobbit of the quiet countryside, expected to find a way where the great ones could not go, or dared not go. It was an evil fate. But he had taken it on himself in his own sitting-room in the far-off spring of another year, so remote now that it was like a chapter in a story of the world's youth, when the Trees of Silver and Gold were still in bloom. This was an evil choice. Which way should he choose? And if both led to terror and death, what good lay in choice?

The day drew on. A deep silence fell upon the little grey hollow where they lay, so near to the borders of the land of fear: a silence that could be felt, as if it were a thick veil that cut them off from all the world about them. Above them was a dome of pale sky barred with fleeting smoke, but it seemed high and far away, as if seen through great deeps of air heavy with brooding thought.

Not even an eagle poised against the sun would have marked the hobbits sitting there, under the weight of doom, silent, not moving, shrouded in their thin grey cloaks. For a moment he might have paused to consider Gollum, a tiny figure sprawling on the ground: there perhaps lay the famished skeleton of some child of Men, its ragged garment still clinging to it, its long arms and legs almost bone-white and bone-thin: no flesh worth a peck.

Frodo's head was bowed over his knees, but Sam leaned back, with hands behind his head, staring out of his hood at the empty sky. At least for a long while it was empty. Then presently Sam thought he saw a dark bird-like figure wheel into the circle of his sight, and hover, and then wheel away again. Two more followed, and then a fourth. They were very small to look at, yet he knew, somehow, that they were huge, with a vast stretch of pinion, flying at a great height. He covered his eyes and bent forward, cowering. The same warning fear was on him as he had felt in the presence of the Black Riders, the helpless horror that had come with the cry in the wind and the shadow on the moon, though now it was not so crushing or compelling: the menace was more remote. But menace it was. Frodo felt it too. His thought was broken. He stirred and shivered, but he did not look up. Gollum huddled himself together like a cornered spider. The winged shapes wheeled, and stooped swiftly down, speeding back to Mordor.

Sam took a deep breath. 'The Riders are about again, up in the air,' he said in a hoarse whisper. 'I saw them. Do you think they could see us? They were very high up. And if they are Black Riders, same as before, then they can't see much by daylight, can they?'

'No, perhaps not,' said Frodo. 'But their steeds could see. And these winged creatures that they ride on now, they can probably see more than any other creature. They are like great carrion birds. They are looking for something: the Enemy is on the watch, I fear.'

The feeling of dread passed, but the enfolding silence was broken. For some time they had been cut off from the world, as if in an invisible island; now they were laid bare again, peril had returned. But still Frodo did not speak to Gollum or make his choice. His eyes were closed, as if he were dreaming, or looking inward into his heart and memory. At last he stirred and stood up, and it seemed that he was about to speak and to decide. But 'hark!' he said. 'What is that?'

A new fear was upon them. They heard singing and hoarse shouting. At first it seemed a long way off, but it drew nearer: it was coming towards them. It leaped into all their minds

that the Black Wings had spied them and had sent armed
soldiers to seize them: no speed seemed too great for these
terrible servants of Sauron. They crouched, listening. The
voices and the clink of weapons and harness were very close.
Frodo and Sam loosened their small swords in their sheaths.
Flight was impossible.

Gollum rose slowly and crawled insect-like to the lip of
the hollow. Very cautiously he raised himself inch by inch,
until he could peer over it between two broken points of
stone. He remained there without moving for some time,
making no sound. Presently the voices began to recede again,
and then they slowly faded away. Far off a horn blew on the
ramparts of the Morannon. Then quietly Gollum drew back
and slipped down into the hollow.

'More Men going to Mordor,' he said in a low voice. 'Dark
faces. We have not seen Men like these before, no, Sméagol
has not. They are fierce. They have black eyes, and long
black hair, and gold rings in their ears; yes, lots of beautiful
gold. And some have red paint on their cheeks, and red
cloaks; and their flags are red, and the tips of their spears;
and they have round shields, yellow and black with big spikes.
Not nice; very cruel wicked Men they look. Almost as bad
as Orcs, and much bigger. Sméagol thinks they have come
out of the South beyond the Great River's end: they came
up that road. They have passed on to the Black Gate; but
more may follow. Always more people coming to Mordor.
One day all the peoples will be inside.'

'Were there any oliphaunts?' asked Sam, forgetting his fear
in his eagerness for news of strange places.

'No, no oliphaunts. What are oliphaunts?' said Gollum.

Sam stood up, putting his hands behind his back (as he
always did when 'speaking poetry'), and began:

> Grey as a mouse,
> Big as a house,
> Nose like a snake,

I make the earth shake,
As I tramp through the grass;
Trees crack as I pass.
With horns in my mouth
I walk in the South,
Flapping big ears.
Beyond count of years
I stump round and round,
Never lie on the ground,
Not even to die.
Oliphaunt am I,
Biggest of all,
Huge, old, and tall.
If ever you'd met me
You wouldn't forget me.
If you never do,
You won't think I'm true;
But old Oliphaunt am I,
And I never lie.

'That,' said Sam, when he had finished reciting, 'that's a rhyme we have in the Shire. Nonsense maybe, and maybe not. But we have our tales too, and news out of the South, you know. In the old days hobbits used to go on their travels now and again. Not that many ever came back, and not that all they said was believed: *news from Bree*, and not *sure as Shiretalk*, as the sayings go. But I've heard tales of the big folk down away in the Sunlands. Swertings we call 'em in our tales; and they ride on oliphaunts, 'tis said, when they fight. They put houses and towers on the oliphauntses backs and all, and the oliphaunts throw rocks and trees at one another. So when you said "Men out of the South, all in red and gold," I said "were there any oliphaunts?" For if there was, I was going to take a look, risk or no. But now I don't suppose I'll ever see an oliphaunt. Maybe there ain't no such a beast.' He sighed.

'No, no oliphaunts,' said Gollum again. 'Sméagol has not

heard of them. He does not want to see them. He does not
want them to be. Sméagol wants to go away from here and
hide somewhere safer. Sméagol wants master to go. Nice
master, won't he come with Sméagol?'

Frodo stood up. He had laughed in the midst of all his
cares when Sam trotted out the old fireside rhyme of *Oliphaunt*, and the laugh had released him from hesitation. 'I
wish we had a thousand oliphaunts with Gandalf on a white
one at their head,' he said. 'Then we'd break a way into this
evil land, perhaps. But we've not; just our own tired legs,
that's all. Well, Sméagol, the third turn may turn the best. I
will come with you.'

'Good master, wise master, nice master!' cried Gollum in
delight, patting Frodo's knees. 'Good master! Then rest now,
nice hobbits, under the shadow of the stones, close under
the stones! Rest and lie quiet, till the Yellow Face goes away.
Then we can go quickly. Soft and quick as shadows we must
be!'

CHAPTER IV

OF HERBS AND STEWED RABBIT

For the few hours of daylight that were left they rested, shifting into the shade as the sun moved, until at last the shadow of the western rim of their dell grew long, and darkness filled all the hollow. Then they ate a little, and drank sparingly. Gollum ate nothing, but he accepted water gladly.

'Soon get more now,' he said, licking his lips. 'Good water runs down in streams to the Great River, nice water in the lands we are going to. Sméagol will get food there too, perhaps. He's very hungry, yes, *gollum!*' He set his two large flat hands on his shrunken belly, and a pale green light came into his eyes.

The dusk was deep when at length they set out, creeping over the westward rim of the dell, and fading like ghosts into the broken country on the borders of the road. The moon was now three nights from the full, but it did not climb over the mountains until nearly midnight, and the early night was very dark. A single red light burned high up in the Towers of the Teeth, but otherwise no sign could be seen or heard of the sleepless watch on the Morannon.

For many miles the red eye seemed to stare at them as they fled, stumbling through a barren stony country. They did not dare to take the road, but they kept it on their left, following its line as well as they could at a little distance. At last, when night was growing old and they were already weary, for they had taken only one short rest, the eye dwindled to a small fiery point and then vanished: they had turned the dark northern shoulder of the lower mountains and were heading southwards.

With hearts strangely lightened they now rested again, but

not for long. They were not going quick enough for Gollum. By his reckoning it was nearly thirty leagues from the Morannon to the cross-roads above Osgiliath, and he hoped to cover that distance in four journeys. So soon they struggled on once more, until the dawn began to spread slowly in the wide grey solitude. They had then walked almost eight leagues, and the hobbits could not have gone any further, even if they had dared.

The growing light revealed to them a land already less barren and ruinous. The mountains still loomed up ominously on their left, but near at hand they could see the southward road, now bearing away from the black roots of the hills and slanting westwards. Beyond it were slopes covered with sombre trees like dark clouds, but all about them lay a tumbled heathland, grown with ling and broom and cornel, and other shrubs that they did not know. Here and there they saw knots of tall pine-trees. The hearts of the hobbits rose again a little in spite of weariness: the air was fresh and fragrant, and it reminded them of the uplands of the Northfarthing far away. It seemed good to be reprieved, to walk in a land that had only been for a few years under the dominion of the Dark Lord and was not yet fallen wholly into decay. But they did not forget their danger, nor the Black Gate that was still all too near, hidden though it was behind the gloomy heights. They looked about for a hiding-place where they could shelter from evil eyes while the light lasted.

The day passed uneasily. They lay deep in the heather and counted out the slow hours, in which there seemed little change; for they were still under the shadows of the Ephel Dúath, and the sun was veiled. Frodo slept at times, deeply and peacefully, either trusting Gollum or too tired to trouble about him; but Sam found it difficult to do more than doze, even when Gollum was plainly fast asleep, whiffling and twitching in his secret dreams. Hunger, perhaps, more than mistrust kept him wakeful: he had begun to long for a good homely meal, 'something hot out of the pot'.

As soon as the land faded into a formless grey under coming night, they started out again. In a little while Gollum led them down on to the southward road; and after that they went on more quickly, though the danger was greater. Their ears were strained for the sound of hoof or foot on the road ahead, or following them from behind; but the night passed, and they heard no sound of walker or rider.

The road had been made in a long lost time, and for perhaps thirty miles below the Morannon it had been newly repaired, but as it went south the wild encroached upon it. The handiwork of Men of old could still be seen in its straight sure flight and level course: now and again it cut its way through hillside slopes, or leaped over a stream upon a wide shapely arch of enduring masonry; but at last all signs of stonework faded, save for a broken pillar here and there, peering out of bushes at the side, or old paving-stones still lurking amid weeds and moss. Heather and trees and bracken scrambled down and overhung the banks, or sprawled out over the surface. It dwindled at last to a country cart-road little used; but it did not wind: it held on its own sure course and guided them by the swiftest way.

So they passed into the northern marches of that land that Men once called Ithilien, a fair country of climbing woods and swift-falling streams. The night became fine under star and round moon, and it seemed to the hobbits that the fragrance of the air grew as they went forward; and from the blowing and muttering of Gollum it seemed that he noticed it too, and did not relish it. At the first signs of day they halted again. They had come to the end of a long cutting, deep, and sheer-sided in the middle, by which the road clove its way through a stony ridge. Now they climbed up the westward bank and looked abroad.

Day was opening in the sky, and they saw that the mountains were now much further off, receding eastward in a long curve that was lost in the distance. Before them, as they turned west, gentle slopes ran down into dim hazes far below. All about them were small woods of resinous trees, fir and cedar and cypress, and other kinds unknown in the Shire, with wide glades among them; and everywhere there was a wealth of sweet-smelling herbs and shrubs. The long journey from Rivendell had brought them far south of their own land, but not until now in this more sheltered region had the hobbits felt the change of clime. Here Spring was already busy about them: fronds pierced moss and mould, larches were green-fingered, small flowers were opening in the turf, birds were singing. Ithilien, the garden of Gondor now desolate kept still a dishevelled dryad loveliness.

South and west it looked towards the warm lower vales of Anduin, shielded from the east by the Ephel Dúath and yet not under the mountain-shadow, protected from the north by the Emyn Muil, open to the southern airs and the moist winds from the Sea far away. Many great trees grew there, planted long ago, falling into untended age amid a riot of careless descendants; and groves and thickets there were of tamarisk and pungent terebinth, of olive and of bay; and there were junipers and myrtles; and thymes that grew in bushes, or with their woody creeping stems mantled in deep tapestries the hidden stones; sages of many kinds putting forth blue flowers, or red, or pale green; and marjorams and new-sprouting parsleys, and many herbs of forms and scents beyond the garden-lore of Sam. The grots and rocky walls were already starred with saxifrages and stonecrops. Primeroles and anemones were awake in the filbert-brakes; and asphodel and many lily-flowers nodded their half-opened heads in the grass: deep green grass beside the pools, where falling streams halted in cool hollows on their journey down to Anduin.

The travellers turned their backs on the road and went downhill. As they walked, brushing their way through bush and herb, sweet odours rose about them. Gollum coughed and retched; but the hobbits breathed deep, and suddenly

Sam laughed, for heart's ease not for jest. They followed a stream that went quickly down before them. Presently it brought them to a small clear lake in a shallow dell: it lay in the broken ruins of an ancient stone basin, the carven rim of which was almost wholly covered with mosses and rose-brambles; iris-swords stood in ranks about it, and water-lily leaves floated on its dark gently-rippling surface; but it was deep and fresh, and spilled ever softly out over a stony lip at the far end.

Here they washed themselves and drank their fill at the in-falling freshet. Then they sought for a resting-place, and a hiding-place; for this land, fair-seeming still, was nonetheless now territory of the Enemy. They had not come very far from the road, and yet even in so short a space they had seen scars of the old wars, and the newer wounds made by the Orcs and other foul servants of the Dark Lord: a pit of uncovered filth and refuse; trees hewn down wantonly and left to die, with evil runes or the fell sign of the Eye cut in rude strokes on their bark.

Sam scrambling below the outfall of the lake, smelling and touching the unfamiliar plants and trees, forgetful for the moment of Mordor, was reminded suddenly of their ever-present peril. He stumbled on a ring still scorched by fire, and in the midst of it he found a pile of charred and broken bones and skulls. The swift growth of the wild with briar and eglantine and trailing clematis was already drawing a veil over this place of dreadful feast and slaughter; but it was not ancient. He hurried back to his companions, but he said nothing: the bones were best left in peace and not pawed and routed by Gollum.

'Let's find a place to lie up in,' he said. 'Not lower down. Higher up for me.'

A little way back above the lake they found a deep brown bed of last year's fern. Beyond it was a thicket of dark-leaved bay-trees climbing up a steep bank that was crowned with old cedars. Here they decided to rest and pass the day, which already promised to be bright and warm. A good day for strolling on their way along the groves and glades of Ithilien; but though Orcs may shun the sunlight, there were too many places here where they could lie hid and watch; and other evil eyes were abroad: Sauron had many servants. Gollum, in any case, would not move under the Yellow Face. Soon it would look over the dark ridges of the Ephel Dúath, and he would faint and cower in the light and heat.

Sam had been giving earnest thought to food as they marched. Now that the despair of the impassable Gate was behind him, he did not feel so inclined as his master to take no thought for their livelihood beyond the end of their errand; and anyway it seemed wiser to him to save the waybread of the Elves for worse times ahead. Six days or more had passed since he reckoned that they had only a bare supply for three weeks.

'If we reach the Fire in that time, we'll be lucky at this rate!' he thought. 'And we might be wanting to get back. We might!'

Besides, at the end of a long night-march, and after bathing and drinking, he felt even more hungry than usual. A supper, or a breakfast, by the fire in the old kitchen at Bagshot Row was what he really wanted. An idea struck him and he turned to Gollum. Gollum had just begun to sneak off on his own, and he was crawling away on all fours through the fern.

'Hi! Gollum!' said Sam. 'Where are you going? Hunting? Well, see here, old noser, you don't like our food, and I'd not be sorry for a change myself. Your new motto's *always ready to help*. Could you find anything fit for a hungry hobbit?'

'Yes, perhaps, yes,' said Gollum. 'Sméagol always helps, if they asks – if they asks nicely.'

'Right!' said Sam. 'I does ask. And if that isn't nice enough, I begs.'

Gollum disappeared. He was away some time, and Frodo after a few mouthfuls of *lembas* settled deep into the brown fern and went to sleep. Sam looked at him. The early daylight was only just creeping down into the shadows under the trees, but he saw his master's face very clearly, and his hands, too, lying at rest on the ground beside him. He was reminded suddenly of Frodo as he had lain, asleep in the house of Elrond, after his deadly wound. Then as he had kept watch Sam had noticed that at times a light seemed to be shining faintly within; but now the light was even clearer and stronger. Frodo's face was peaceful, the marks of fear and care had left it; but it looked old, old and beautiful, as if the chiselling of the shaping years was now revealed in many fine lines that had before been hidden, though the identity of the face was not changed. Not that Sam Gamgee put it that way to himself. He shook his head, as if finding words useless, and murmured: 'I love him. He's like that, and sometimes it shines through, somehow. But I love him, whether or no.'

Gollum returned quietly and peered over Sam's shoulder. Looking at Frodo, he shut his eyes and crawled away without a sound. Sam came to him a moment later and found him chewing something and muttering to himself. On the ground beside him lay two small rabbits, which he was beginning to eye greedily.

'Sméagol always helps,' he said. 'He has brought rabbits, nice rabbits. But master has gone to sleep, and perhaps Sam wants to sleep. Doesn't want rabbits now? Sméagol tries to help, but he can't catch things all in a minute.'

Sam, however, had no objection to rabbit at all, and said so. At least not to cooked rabbit. All hobbits, of course, can cook, for they begin to learn the art before their letters (which many never reach); but Sam was a good cook, even by hobbit reckoning, and he had done a good deal of the camp-cooking on their travels, when there was a chance. He still hopefully carried some of his gear in his pack: a small tinder-box, two small shallow pans, the smaller fitting into the larger; inside them a wooden spoon, a short two-pronged fork and some skewers were stowed; and hidden at the bottom of the pack in a flat wooden box a dwindling treasure, some salt. But he needed a fire, and other things besides. He thought for a bit, while he took out his knife, cleaned and whetted it, and began to dress the rabbits. He was not going to leave Frodo alone asleep even for a few minutes.

'Now, Gollum,' he said, 'I've another job for you. Go and fill these pans with water, and bring 'em back!'

'Sméagol will fetch water, yes,' said Gollum. 'But what does the hobbit want all that water for? He has drunk, he has washed.'

'Never you mind,' said Sam. 'If you can't guess, you'll soon find out. And the sooner you fetch the water, the sooner you'll learn. Don't you damage one of my pans, or I'll carve you into mincemeat.'

While Gollum was away Sam took another look at Frodo. He was still sleeping quietly, but Sam was now struck most by the leanness of his face and hands. 'Too thin and drawn he is,' he muttered. 'Not right for a hobbit. If I can get these coneys cooked, I'm going to wake him up.'

Sam gathered a pile of the driest fern, and then scrambled up the bank collecting a bundle of twigs and broken wood; the fallen branch of a cedar at the top gave him a good supply. He cut out some turves at the foot of the bank just outside the fern-brake, and made a shallow hole and laid his fuel in it. Being handy with flint and tinder he soon had a small blaze going. It made little or no smoke but gave off an aromatic scent. He was just stooping over his fire, shielding it and building it up with heavier wood, when Gollum returned, carrying the pans carefully and grumbling to himself.

He set the pans down, and then suddenly saw what Sam was doing. He gave a thin hissing shriek, and seemed to be both frightened and angry. 'Ach! Sss – no!' he cried. 'No! Silly hobbits, foolish, yes foolish! They mustn't do it!'

'Mustn't do what?' asked Sam in surprise.

'Not make the nassty red tongues,' hissed Gollum. 'Fire, fire! It's dangerous, yes it is. It burns, it kills. And it will bring enemies, yes it will.'

'I don't think so,' said Sam. 'Don't see why it should, if you don't put wet stuff on it and make a smother. But if it does, it does. I'm going to risk it, anyhow. I'm going to stew these coneys.'

'Stew the rabbits!' squealed Gollum in dismay. 'Spoil beautiful meat Sméagol saved for you, poor hungry Sméagol! What for? What for, silly hobbit? They are young, they are tender, they are nice. Eat them, eat them!' He clawed at the nearest rabbit, already skinned and lying by the fire.

'Now, now!' said Sam. 'Each to his own fashion. Our bread chokes you, and raw coney chokes me. If you give me a coney, the coney's mine, see, to cook, if I have a mind. And I have. You needn't watch me. Go and catch another and eat it as you fancy – somewhere private and out o' my sight. Then you won't see the fire, and I shan't see you, and we'll both be the happier. I'll see the fire don't smoke, if that's any comfort to you.'

Gollum withdrew grumbling, and crawled into the fern. Sam busied himself with his pans. 'What a hobbit needs with coney,' he said to himself, 'is some herbs and roots, especially taters – not to mention bread. Herbs we can manage, seemingly.'

'Gollum!' he called softly. 'Third time pays for all. I want some herbs.' Gollum's head peeped out of the fern, but his looks were neither helpful nor friendly. 'A few bay-leaves, some thyme and sage, will do – before the water boils,' said Sam.

'No!' said Gollum. 'Sméagol is not pleased. And Sméagol doesn't like smelly leaves. He doesn't eat grasses or roots, no precious, not till he's starving or very sick, poor Sméagol.'

'Sméagol'll get into real true hot water, when this water boils, if he don't do as he's asked,' growled Sam. 'Sam'll put his head in it, yes precious. And I'd make him look for turnips and carrots, and taters too, if it was the time o' the year. I'll bet there's all sorts of good things running wild in this country. I'd give a lot for half a dozen taters.'

'Sméagol won't go, O no precious, not this time,' hissed

Gollum. 'He's frightened, and he's very tired, and this hob-bit's not nice, not nice at all. Sméagol won't grub for roots and carrotses and – taters. What's taters, precious, eh, what's taters?'

'Po – ta – toes,' said Sam. 'The Gaffer's delight, and rare good ballast for an empty belly. But you won't find any, so you needn't look. But be good Sméagol and fetch me the herbs, and I'll think better of you. What's more, if you turn over a new leaf, and keep it turned, I'll cook you some taters one of these days. I will: fried fish and chips served by S. Gamgee. You couldn't say no to that.'

'Yes, yes we could. Spoiling nice fish, scorching it. Give me fish *now*, and keep nassty chips!'

'Oh you're hopeless,' said Sam. 'Go to sleep!'

In the end he had to find what he wanted for himself; but he did not have to go far, not out of sight of the place where his master lay, still sleeping. For a while Sam sat musing, and tending the fire till the water boiled. The daylight grew and the air became warm; the dew faded off turf and leaf. Soon the rabbits cut up lay simmering in their pans with the bunched herbs. Almost Sam fell asleep as the time went by. He let them stew for close on an hour, testing them now and again with his fork, and tasting the broth.

When he thought all was ready he lifted the pans off the fire, and crept along to Frodo. Frodo half opened his eyes as Sam stood over him, and then he wakened from his dream-ing: another gentle, unrecoverable dream of peace.

'Hullo, Sam!' he said. 'Not resting? Is anything wrong? What is the time?'

'About a couple of hours after daybreak,' said Sam, 'and nigh on half past eight by Shire clocks, maybe. But nothing's wrong. Though it ain't quite what I'd call right: no stock, no onions, no taters. I've got a bit of a stew for you, and some broth, Mr. Frodo. Do you good. You'll have to sup it in your mug; or straight from the pan, when it's cooled a bit. I haven't brought no bowls, nor nothing proper.'

Frodo yawned and stretched. 'You should have been rest-ing, Sam,' he said. 'And lighting a fire was dangerous in these parts. But I do feel hungry. Hmm! Can I smell it from here? What have you stewed?'

'A present from Sméagol,' said Sam: 'a brace o' young coneys; though I fancy Gollum's regretting them now. But there's nought to go with them but a few herbs.'

Sam and his master sat just within the fern-brake and ate their stew from the pans, sharing the old fork and spoon. They allowed themselves half a piece of the Elvish waybread each. It seemed a feast.

'Wheew! Gollum!' Sam called and whistled softly. 'Come on! Still time to change your mind. There's some left, if you want to try stewed coney.' There was no answer.

'Oh well, I suppose he's gone off to find something for himself. We'll finish it,' said Sam.

'And then you must take some sleep,' said Frodo.

'Don't you drop off, while I'm nodding, Mr. Frodo. I don't feel too sure of him. There's a good deal of Stinker – the bad Gollum, if you understand me – in him still, and it's getting stronger again. Not but what I think he'd try to throttle me first now. We don't see eye to eye, and he's not pleased with Sam, O no precious, not pleased at all.'

They finished, and Sam went off to the stream to rinse his gear. As he stood up to return, he looked back up the slope. At that moment he saw the sun rise out of the reek, or haze, or dark shadow, or whatever it was, that lay ever to the east, and it sent its golden beams down upon the trees and glades about him. Then he noticed a thin spiral of blue-grey smoke, plain to see as it caught the sunlight, rising from a thicket above him. With a shock he realized that this was the smoke from his little cooking-fire, which he had neglected to put out.

'That won't do! Never thought it would show like that!' he muttered, and he started to hurry back. Suddenly he halted

and listened. Had he heard a whistle or not? Or was it the
call of some strange bird? If it was a whistle, it did not come
from Frodo's direction. There it went again from another
place! Sam began to run as well as he could uphill.

He found that a small brand, burning away to its outer
end, had kindled some fern at the edge of the fire, and the
fern blazing up had set the turves smouldering. Hastily he
stamped out what was left of the fire, scattered the ashes,
and laid the turves on the hole. Then he crept back to Frodo.

'Did you hear a whistle, and what sounded like an answer?'
he asked. 'A few minutes back. I hope it was only a bird, but
it didn't sound quite like that: more like somebody mimicking
a bird-call, I thought. And I'm afraid my bit of fire's been
smoking. Now if I've gone and brought trouble, I'll never
forgive myself. Nor won't have a chance, maybe!'

'Hush!' whispered Frodo. 'I thought I heard voices.'

The two hobbits trussed their small packs, put them on
ready for flight, and then crawled deeper into the fern. There
they crouched listening.

There was no doubt of the voices. They were speaking
low and furtively, but they were near, and coming nearer.
Then quite suddenly one spoke clearly close at hand.

'Here! Here is where the smoke came from!' it said. ''Twill
be nigh at hand. In the fern, no doubt. We shall have it like
a coney in a trap. Then we shall learn what kind of thing it
is.'

'Aye, and what it knows!' said a second voice.

At once four men came striding through the fern from
different directions. Since flight and hiding were no longer
possible, Frodo and Sam sprang to their feet, putting back
to back and whipping out their small swords.

If they were astonished at what they saw, their captors
were even more astonished. Four tall Men stood there. Two
had spears in their hands with broad bright heads. Two had
great bows, almost of their own height, and great quivers of
long green-feathered arrows. All had swords at their sides,

and were clad in green and brown of varied hues, as if the better to walk unseen in the glades of Ithilien. Green gauntlets covered their hands, and their faces were hooded and masked with green, except for their eyes, which were very keen and bright. At once Frodo thought of Boromir, for these Men were like him in stature and bearing, and in their manner of speech.

'We have not found what we sought,' said one. 'But what have we found?'

'Not Orcs,' said another, releasing the hilt of his sword, which he had seized when he saw the glitter of Sting in Frodo's hand.

'Elves?' said a third, doubtfully.

'Nay! Not Elves,' said the fourth, the tallest, and as it appeared the chief among them. 'Elves do not walk in Ithilien in these days. And Elves are wondrous fair to look upon, or so 'tis said.'

'Meaning we're not, I take you,' said Sam. 'Thank you kindly. And when you've finished discussing us, perhaps you'll say who *you* are, and why you can't let two tired travellers rest.'

The tall green man laughed grimly. 'I am Faramir, Captain of Gondor,' he said. 'But there are no travellers in this land: only the servants of the Dark Tower, or of the White.'

'But we are neither,' said Frodo. 'And travellers we are, whatever Captain Faramir may say.'

'Then make haste to declare yourselves and your errand,' said Faramir. 'We have a work to do, and this is no time or place for riddling or parleying. Come! Where is the third of your company?'

'The third?'

'Yes, the skulking fellow that we saw with his nose in the pool down yonder. He had an ill-favoured look. Some spying breed of Orc, I guess, or a creature of theirs. But he gave us the slip by some fox-trick.'

'I do not know where he is,' said Frodo. 'He is only a chance companion met upon our road, and I am not answerable for him. If you come on him, spare him. Bring him or send him to us. He is only a wretched gangrel creature, but I have him under my care for a while. But as for us, we are Hobbits of the Shire, far to the North and West, beyond many rivers. Frodo son of Drogo is my name, and with me is Samwise son of Hamfast, a worthy hobbit in my service. We have come by long ways – out of Rivendell, or Imladris as some call it.' Here Faramir started and grew intent. 'Seven companions we had: one we lost at Moria, the others we left at Parth Galen above Rauros: two of my kin; a Dwarf there was also, and an Elf, and two Men. They were Aragorn; and Boromir, who said that he came out of Minas Tirith, a city in the South.'

'Boromir!' all the four men exclaimed.

'Boromir son of the Lord Denethor?' said Faramir, and a strange stern look came into his face. 'You came with him? That is news indeed, if it be true. Know, little strangers, that Boromir son of Denethor was High Warden of the White Tower, and our Captain-General: sorely do we miss him. Who are you then, and what had you to do with him? Be swift, for the Sun is climbing!'

'Are the riddling words known to you that Boromir brought to Rivendell?' Frodo replied.

> Seek for the Sword that was Broken.
> In Imladris it dwells.

'The words are known indeed,' said Faramir in astonishment. 'It is some token of your truth that you also know them.'

'Aragorn whom I named is the bearer of the Sword that was Broken,' said Frodo. 'And we are the Halflings that the rhyme spoke of.'

'That I see,' said Faramir thoughtfully. 'Or I see that it might be so. And what is Isildur's Bane?'

'That is hidden,' answered Frodo. 'Doubtless it will be made clear in time.'

'We must learn more of this,' said Faramir, 'and know what brings you so far east under the shadow of yonder————,' he pointed and said no name. 'But not now. We have business in hand. You are in peril, and you would not have gone far by field or road this day. There will be hard handstrokes nigh at hand ere the day is full. Then death, or swift flight back to Anduin. I will leave two to guard you, for your good and for mine. Wise man trusts not to chance-meeting on the road in this land. If I return, I will speak more with you.'

'Farewell!' said Frodo, bowing low. 'Think what you will, I am a friend of all enemies of the One Enemy. We would go with you, if we halfling folk could hope to serve you, such doughty men and strong as you seem, and if my errand permitted it. May the light shine on your swords!'

'The Halflings are courteous folk, whatever else they be,' said Faramir. 'Farewell!'

The hobbits sat down again, but they said nothing to one another of their thoughts and doubts. Close by, just under the dappling shadow of the dark bay-trees, two men remained on guard. They took off their masks now and again to cool them, as the day-heat grew, and Frodo saw that they were goodly men, pale-skinned, dark of hair, with grey eyes and faces sad and proud. They spoke together in soft voices, at first using the Common Speech, but after the manner of older days, and then changing to another language of their own. To his amazement, as he listened Frodo became aware that it was the Elven-tongue that they spoke, or one but little different; and he looked at them with wonder, for he knew then that they must be Dúnedain of the South, men of the line of the Lords of Westernesse.

After a while he spoke to them; but they were slow and cautious in answering. They named themselves Mablung and Damrod, soldiers of Gondor, and they were Rangers of Ithil-ien; for they were descended from folk who lived in Ithilien at one time, before it was overrun. From such men the Lord Denethor chose his forayers, who crossed the Anduin secretly (how or where, they would not say) to harry the Orcs and other enemies that roamed between the Ephel Dúath and the River.

'It is close on ten leagues hence to the east-shore of Anduin,' said Mablung, 'and we seldom come so far afield. But we have a new errand on this journey: we come to ambush the Men of Harad. Curse them!'

'Aye, curse the Southrons!' said Damrod. ''Tis said that there were dealings of old between Gondor and the kingdoms of the Harad in the Far South; though there was never friendship. In those days our bounds were away south beyond the mouths of Anduin, and Umbar, the nearest of their realms, acknowledged our sway. But that is long since. 'Tis many lives of Men since any passed to or fro between us. Now of late we have learned that the Enemy has been among them, and they are gone over to Him, or back to Him – they were ever ready to His will – as have so many also in the East. I doubt not that the days of Gondor are numbered, and the walls of Minas Tirith are doomed, so great is His strength and malice.'

'But still we will not sit idle and let Him do all as He would,' said Mablung. 'These cursed Southrons come now marching up the ancient roads to swell the hosts of the Dark Tower. Yea, up the very roads that craft of Gondor made. And they go ever more heedlessly, we learn, thinking that the power of their new master is great enough, so that the mere shadow of His hills will protect them. We come to teach them another lesson. Great strength of them was reported to us some days ago, marching north. One of their regiments is due by our reckoning to pass by, some time ere noon – up on the road above, where it passes through the cloven way. The road may pass, but they shall not! Not while Faramir is Captain. He leads now in all perilous ventures. But his life is charmed, or fate spares him for some other end.'

Their talk died down into a listening silence. All seemed still and watchful. Sam, crouched by the edge of the fern-brake, peered out. With his keen hobbit-eyes he saw that many more Men were about. He could see them stealing up the slopes, singly or in long files, keeping always to the shade of grove or thicket, or crawling, hardly visible in their brown and green raiment, through grass and brake. All were hooded and masked, and had gauntlets on their hands, and were armed like Faramir and his companions. Before long they had all passed and vanished. The sun rose till it neared the South. The shadows shrank.

'I wonder where that dratted Gollum is?' thought Sam, as he crawled back into deeper shade. 'He stands a fair chance of being spitted for an Orc, or of being roasted by the Yellow Face. But I fancy he'll look after himself.' He lay down beside Frodo and began to doze.

He woke, thinking that he had heard horns blowing. He sat up. It was now high noon. The guards stood alert and tense in the shadow of the trees. Suddenly the horns rang out louder and beyond mistake from above, over the top of the slope. Sam thought that he heard cries and wild shouting also, but the sound was faint, as if it came out of some distant cave. Then presently the noise of fighting broke out near at hand, just above their hiding-place. He could hear plainly the ringing grate of steel on steel, the clang of sword on iron cap, the dull beat of blade on shield; men were yelling and screaming, and one clear loud voice was calling *Gondor! Gondor!*

'It sounds like a hundred blacksmiths all smithying together,' said Sam to Frodo. 'They're as near as I want them now.'

But the noise grew closer. 'They are coming!' cried Damrod. 'See! Some of the Southrons have broken from the trap and are flying from the road. There they go! Our men after them, and the Captain leading.'

Sam, eager to see more, went now and joined the guards. He scrambled a little way up into one of the larger of the bay-trees. For a moment he caught a glimpse of swarthy men in red running down the slope some way off with green-clad warriors leaping after them, hewing them down as they fled. Arrows were thick in the air. Then suddenly straight over the rim of their sheltering bank, a man fell, crashing through the slender trees, nearly on top of them. He came to rest in the fern a few feet away, face downward, green arrow-feathers sticking from his neck below a golden collar. His scarlet robes were tattered, his corslet of overlapping brazen plates was rent and hewn, his black plaits of hair braided with gold were drenched with blood. His brown hand still clutched the hilt of a broken sword.

It was Sam's first view of a battle of Men against Men, and he did not like it much. He was glad that he could not see the dead face. He wondered what the man's name was and where he came from; and if he was really evil of heart, or what lies or threats had led him on the long march from his home; and if he would not really rather have stayed there in peace – all in a flash of thought which was quickly driven from his mind. For just as Mablung stepped towards the fallen body, there was a new noise. Great crying and shouting. Amidst it Sam heard a shrill bellowing or trumpeting. And then a great thudding and bumping, like huge rams dinning on the ground.

'Ware! Ware!' cried Damrod to his companion. 'May the Valar turn him aside! Mûmak! Mûmak!'

To his astonishment and terror, and lasting delight, Sam saw a vast shape crash out of the trees and come careering down the slope. Big as a house, much bigger than a house, it looked to him, a grey-clad moving hill. Fear and wonder, maybe, enlarged him in the hobbit's eyes, but the Mûmak of Harad was indeed a beast of vast bulk, and the like of him does not walk now in Middle-earth; his kin that live still in latter days are but memories of his girth and majesty. On he came, straight towards the watchers, and then swerved aside in the nick of time, passing only a few yards away, rocking the ground beneath their feet: his great legs like trees, enormous sail-like ears spread out, long snout upraised like a huge serpent about to strike, his small red eyes raging. His upturned hornlike tusks were bound with bands of gold and dripped with blood. His trappings of scarlet and gold flapped about him in wild tatters. The ruins of what seemed a very war-tower lay upon his heaving back, smashed in his furious passage through the woods; and high upon his neck still desperately clung a tiny figure – the body of a mighty warrior, a giant among the Swertings.

On the great beast thundered, blundering in blind wrath through pool and thicket. Arrows skipped and snapped harmlessly about the triple hide of his flanks. Men of both sides fled before him, but many he overtook and crushed to the ground. Soon he was lost to view, still trumpeting and stamping far away. What became of him Sam never heard: whether he escaped to roam the wild for a time, until he perished far from his home or was trapped in some deep pit; or whether he raged on until he plunged in the Great River and was swallowed up.

Sam drew a deep breath. 'An Oliphaunt it was!' he said. 'So there are Oliphaunts, and I have seen one. What a life! But no one at home will ever believe me. Well, if that's over, I'll have a bit of sleep.'

'Sleep while you may,' said Mablung. 'But the Captain will return, if he is unhurt; and when he comes we shall depart swiftly. We shall be pursued as soon as news of our deed reaches the Enemy, and that will not be long.'

'Go quietly when you must!' said Sam. 'No need to disturb my sleep. I was walking all night.'

Mablung laughed. 'I do not think the Captain will leave you here, Master Samwise,' he said. 'But you shall see.'

CHAPTER V

THE WINDOW ON THE WEST

It seemed to Sam that he had only dozed for a few minutes when he awoke to find that it was late afternoon and Faramir had come back. He had brought many men with him; indeed all the survivors of the foray were now gathered on the slope nearby, two or three hundred strong. They sat in a wide semicircle, between the arms of which Faramir was seated on the ground, while Frodo stood before him. It looked strangely like the trial of a prisoner.

Sam crept out from the fern, but no one paid any attention to him, and he placed himself at the end of the rows of men, where he could see and hear all that was going on. He watched and listened intently, ready to dash to his master's aid if needed. He could see Faramir's face, which was now unmasked: it was stern and commanding, and a keen wit lay behind his searching glance. Doubt was in the grey eyes that gazed steadily at Frodo.

Sam soon became aware that the Captain was not satisfied with Frodo's account of himself at several points: what part he had to play in the Company that set out from Rivendell; why he had left Boromir; and where he was now going. In particular he returned often to Isildur's Bane. Plainly he saw that Frodo was concealing from him some matter of great importance.

'But it was at the coming of the Halfling that Isildur's Bane should waken, or so one must read the words,' he insisted. 'If then you are the Halfling that was named, doubtless you brought this thing, whatever it may be, to the Council of which you speak, and there Boromir saw it. Do you deny it?'

Frodo made no answer. 'So!' said Faramir. 'I wish then to

learn from you more of it; for what concerns Boromir concerns me. An orc-arrow slew Isildur, so far as old tales tell. But orc-arrows are plenty, and the sight of one would not be taken as a sign of Doom by Boromir of Gondor. Had you this thing in keeping? It is hidden, you say; but is not that because you choose to hide it?'

'No, not because I choose,' answered Frodo. 'It does not belong to me. It does not belong to any mortal, great or small; though if any could claim it, it would be Aragorn son of Arathorn, whom I named, the leader of our Company from Moria to Rauros.'

'Why so, and not Boromir, prince of the City that the sons of Elendil founded?'

'Because Aragorn is descended in direct lineage, father to father, from Isildur Elendil's son himself. And the sword that he bears was Elendil's sword.'

A murmur of astonishment ran through all the ring of men. Some cried aloud: 'The sword of Elendil! The sword of Elendil comes to Minas Tirith! Great tidings!' But Faramir's face was unmoved.

'Maybe,' he said. 'But so great a claim will need to be established, and clear proofs will be required, should this Aragorn ever come to Minas Tirith. He had not come, nor any of your Company, when I set out six days ago.'

'Boromir was satisfied of that claim,' said Frodo. 'Indeed, if Boromir were here, he would answer all your questions. And since he was already at Rauros many days back, and intended then to go straight to your city, if you return, you may soon learn the answers there. My part in the Company was known to him, as to all the others, for it was appointed to me by Elrond of Imladris himself before the whole Council. On that errand I came into this country, but it is not mine to reveal to any outside the Company. Yet those who claim to oppose the Enemy would do well not to hinder it.'

Frodo's tone was proud, whatever he felt, and Sam approved of it; but it did not appease Faramir.

'So!' he said. 'You bid me mind my own affairs, and get

me back home, and let you be. Boromir will tell all, when he comes. When he comes, say you! Were you a friend of Boromir?'

Vividly before Frodo's mind came the memory of Boromir's assault upon him, and for a moment he hesitated. Faramir's eyes watching him grew harder. 'Boromir was a valiant member of our Company,' said Frodo at length. 'Yes, I was his friend, for my part.'

Faramir smiled grimly. 'Then you would grieve to learn that Boromir is dead?'

'I would grieve indeed,' said Frodo. Then catching the look in Faramir's eyes, he faltered. 'Dead?' he said. 'Do you mean that he is dead, and that you knew it? You have been trying to trap me in words, playing with me? Or are you now trying to snare me with a falsehood?'

'I would not snare even an orc with a falsehood,' said Faramir.

'How then did he die, and how do you know of it? Since you say that none of the Company had reached the city when you left.'

'As to the manner of his death, I had hoped that his friend and companion would tell me how it was.'

'But he was alive and strong when we parted. And he lives still for all that I know. Though surely there are many perils in the world.'

'Many indeed,' said Faramir, 'and treachery not the least.'

Sam had been getting more and more impatient and angry at this conversation. These last words were more than he could bear, and bursting into the middle of the ring, he strode up to his master's side.

'Begging your pardon, Mr. Frodo,' he said, 'but this has gone on long enough. He's no right to talk to you so. After all you've gone through, as much for his good and all these great Men as for anyone else.

'See here, Captain!' He planted himself squarely in front

of Faramir, his hands on his hips, and a look on his face as if he was addressing a young hobbit who had offered him what he called 'sauce' when questioned about visits to the orchard. There was some murmuring, but also some grins on the faces of the men looking on: the sight of their Captain sitting on the ground and eye to eye with a young hobbit, legs well apart, bristling with wrath, was one beyond their experience. 'See here!' he said. 'What are you driving at? Let's come to the point before all the Orcs of Mordor come down on us! If you think my master murdered this Boromir and then ran away, you've got no sense; but say it, and have done! And then let us know what you mean to do about it. But it's a pity that folk as talk about fighting the Enemy can't let others do their bit in their own way without interfering. He'd be mighty pleased, if he could see you now. Think he'd got a new friend, he would.'

'Patience!' said Faramir, but without anger. 'Do not speak before your master, whose wit is greater than yours. And I do not need any to teach me of our peril. Even so, I spare a brief time, in order to judge justly in a hard matter. Were I as hasty as you, I might have slain you long ago. For I am commanded to slay all whom I find in this land without the leave of the Lord of Gondor. But I do not slay man or beast needlessly, and not gladly even when it is needed. Neither do I talk in vain. So be comforted. Sit by your master, and be silent!'

Sam sat down heavily with a red face. Faramir turned to Frodo again. 'You asked how do I know that the son of Denethor is dead. Tidings of death have many wings. *Night oft brings news to near kindred*, 'tis said. Boromir was my brother.'

A shadow of sorrow passed over his face. 'Do you remember aught of special mark that the Lord Boromir bore with him among his gear?'

Frodo thought for a moment, fearing some further trap, and wondering how this debate would turn in the end. He had hardly saved the Ring from the proud grasp of Boromir,

and how he would fare now among so many men, warlike
and strong, he did not know. Yet he felt in his heart that
Faramir, though he was much like his brother in looks, was
a man less self-regarding, both sterner and wiser. 'I remember
that Boromir bore a horn,' he said at last.

'You remember well, and as one who has in truth seen
him,' said Faramir. 'Then maybe you can see it in your
mind's eye: a great horn of the wild ox of the East, bound
with silver, and written with ancient characters. That horn
the eldest son of our house has borne for many generations;
and it is said that if it be blown at need anywhere within the
bounds of Gondor, as the realm was of old, its voice will not
pass unheeded.

'Five days ere I set out on this venture, eleven days ago at
about this hour of the day, I heard the blowing of that horn:
from the northward it seemed, but dim, as if it were but an
echo in the mind. A boding of ill we thought it, my father
and I, for no tidings had we heard of Boromir since he went
away, and no watcher on our borders had seen him pass.
And on the third night after another and a stranger thing
befell me.

'I sat at night by the waters of Anduin, in the grey dark
under the young pale moon, watching the ever-moving
stream; and the sad reeds were rustling. So do we ever watch
the shores nigh Osgiliath, which our enemies now partly hold,
and issue from it to harry our lands. But that night all the
world slept at the midnight hour. Then I saw, or it seemed
that I saw, a boat floating on the water, glimmering grey, a
small boat of a strange fashion with a high prow, and there
was none to row or steer it.

'An awe fell on me, for a pale light was round it. But I
rose and went to the bank, and began to walk out into the
stream, for I was drawn towards it. Then the boat turned
towards me, and stayed its pace, and floated slowly by within
my hand's reach, yet I durst not handle it. It waded deep, as
if it were heavily burdened, and it seemed to me as it passed
under my gaze that it was almost filled with clear water, from

which came the light; and lapped in the water a warrior lay asleep.

'A broken sword was on his knee. I saw many wounds on him. It was Boromir, my brother, dead. I knew his gear, his sword, his beloved face. One thing only I missed: his horn. One thing only I knew not: a fair belt, as it were of linked golden leaves, about his waist. *Boromir!* I cried. *Where is thy horn? Whither goest thou? O Boromir!* But he was gone. The boat turned into the stream and passed glimmering on into the night. Dreamlike it was, and yet no dream, for there was no waking. And I do not doubt that he is dead and has passed down the River to the Sea.'

'Alas!' said Frodo. 'That was indeed Boromir as I knew him. For the golden belt was given to him in Lothlórien by the Lady Galadriel. She it was that clothed us as you see us, in elven-grey. This brooch is of the same workmanship.' He touched the green and silver leaf that fastened his cloak beneath his throat.

Faramir looked closely at it. 'It is beautiful,' he said. 'Yes, 'tis work of the same craft. So then you passed through the Land of Lórien? Laurelindórenan it was named of old, but long now it has lain beyond the knowledge of Men,' he added softly, regarding Frodo with a new wonder in his eyes. 'Much that was strange about you I begin now to understand. Will you not tell me more? For it is a bitter thought that Boromir died, within sight of the land of his home.'

'No more can I say than I have said,' answered Frodo. 'Though your tale fills me with foreboding. A vision it was that you saw, I think, and no more, some shadow of evil fortune that has been or will be. Unless indeed it is some lying trick of the Enemy. I have seen the faces of fair warriors of old laid in sleep beneath the pools of the Dead Marshes, or seeming so by his foul arts.'

'Nay, it was not so,' said Faramir. 'For his works fill the heart with loathing; but my heart was filled with grief and pity.'

'Yet how could such a thing have happened in truth?' asked Frodo. 'For no boat could have been carried over the stony hills from Tol Brandir; and Boromir purposed to go home across the Entwash and the fields of Rohan. And yet how could any vessel ride the foam of the great falls and not founder in the boiling pools, though laden with water?'

'I know not,' said Faramir. 'But whence came the boat?'

'From Lórien,' said Frodo. 'In three such boats we rowed down Anduin to the Falls. They also were of elven-work.'

'You passed through the Hidden Land,' said Faramir, 'but it seems that you little understood its power. If Men have dealings with the Mistress of Magic who dwells in the Golden Wood, then they may look for strange things to follow. For it is perilous for mortal man to walk out of the world of this Sun, and few of old came thence unchanged, 'tis said.

'*Boromir, O Boromir!*' he cried. '*What did she say to you, the Lady that dies not? What did she see? What woke in your heart then? Why went you ever to Laurelindórenan, and came not by your own road, upon the horses of Rohan riding home in the morning?*'

Then turning again to Frodo, he spoke in a quiet voice once more. 'To those questions I guess that you could make some answer, Frodo son of Drogo. But not here or now, maybe. But lest you still should think my tale a vision, I will tell you this. The horn of Boromir at least returned in truth, and not in seeming. The horn came, but it was cloven in two, as it were by axe or sword. The shards came severally to shore: one was found among the reeds where watchers of Gondor lay, northwards below the infalls of the Entwash; the other was found spinning on the flood by one who had an errand on the water. Strange chances, but murder will out, 'tis said.

'And now the horn of the elder son lies in two pieces upon the lap of Denethor, sitting in his high chair, waiting for news. And you can tell me nothing of the cleaving of the horn?'

'No, I did not know of it,' said Frodo. 'But the day when

you heard it blowing, if your reckoning is true, was the day when we parted, when I and my servant left the Company. And now your tale fills me with dread. For if Boromir was then in peril and was slain, I must fear that all my companions perished too. And they were my kindred and my friends.

'Will you not put aside your doubt of me and let me go? I am weary, and full of grief, and afraid. But I have a deed to do, or to attempt, before I too am slain. And the more need of haste, if we two halflings are all that remain of our fellowship.

'Go back, Faramir, valiant Captain of Gondor, and defend your city while you may, and let me go where my doom takes me.'

'For me there is no comfort in our speech together,' said Faramir; 'but you surely draw from it more dread than need be. Unless the people of Lórien themselves came to him, who arrayed Boromir as for a funeral? Not Orcs or servants of the Nameless. Some of your Company, I guess, live still.

'But whatever befell on the North March, you, Frodo, I doubt no longer. If hard days have made me any judge of Men's words and faces, then I may make a guess at Halflings! Though,' and now he smiled, 'there is something strange about you, Frodo, an elvish air, maybe. But more lies upon our words together than I thought at first. I should now take you back to Minas Tirith to answer there to Denethor, and my life will justly be forfeit, if I now choose a course that proves ill for my city. So I will not decide in haste what is to be done. Yet we must move hence without more delay.'

He sprang to his feet and issued some orders. At once the men who were gathered round him broke up into small groups, and went off this way and that, vanishing quickly into the shadows of the rocks and trees. Soon only Mablung and Damrod remained.

'Now you, Frodo and Samwise, will come with me and my guards,' said Faramir. 'You cannot go along the road southwards, if that was your purpose. It will be unsafe for some days, and always more closely watched after this affray than it has been yet. And you cannot, I think, go far today in any case, for you are weary. And so are we. We are going now to a secret place we have, somewhat less than ten miles from here. The Orcs and spies of the Enemy have not found it yet, and if they did, we could hold it long even against many. There we may lie up and rest for a while, and you with us. In the morning I will decide what is best for me to do, and for you.'

There was nothing for Frodo to do but to fall in with this request, or order. It seemed in any case a wise course for the moment, since this foray of the men of Gondor had made a journey in Ithilien more dangerous than ever.

They set out at once: Mablung and Damrod a little ahead, and Faramir with Frodo and Sam behind. Skirting the hither side of the pool where the hobbits had bathed, they crossed the stream, climbed a long bank, and passed into green-shadowed woodlands that marched ever downwards and westwards. While they walked, as swiftly as the hobbits could go, they talked in hushed voices.

'I broke off our speech together,' said Faramir, 'not only because time pressed, as Master Samwise had reminded me, but also because we were drawing near to matters that were better not debated openly before many men. It was for that reason that I turned rather to the matter of my brother and let be *Isildur's Bane*. You were not wholly frank with me, Frodo.'

'I told no lies, and of the truth all I could,' said Frodo.

'I do not blame you,' said Faramir. 'You spoke with skill in a hard place, and wisely, it seemed to me. But I learned or guessed more from you than your words said. You were not friendly with Boromir, or you did not part in friendship. You, and Master Samwise, too, I guess have some grievance. Now I loved him dearly, and would gladly avenge his death, yet I knew him well. *Isildur's Bane* – I would hazard that *Isildur's Bane* lay between you and was a cause of contention in your Company. Clearly it is a mighty heirloom of some sort, and such things do not breed peace among confederates, not if aught may be learned from ancient tales. Do I not hit near the mark?'

'Near,' said Frodo, 'but not in the gold. There was no contention in our Company, though there was doubt: doubt which way we should take from the Emyn Muil. But be that as it may, ancient tales teach us also the peril of rash words concerning such things as – heirlooms.'

'Ah, then it is as I thought: your trouble was with Boromir alone. He wished this thing brought to Minas Tirith. Alas! it is a crooked fate that seals your lips who saw him last, and holds from me that which I long to know: what was in his heart and thought in his latest hours. Whether he erred or no, of this I am sure: he died well, achieving some good thing. His face was more beautiful even than in life.

'But, Frodo, I pressed you hard at first about *Isildur's Bane*. Forgive me! It was unwise in such an hour and place. I had not had time for thought. We had had a hard fight, and there was more than enough to fill my mind. But even as I spoke with you, I drew nearer to the mark, and so deliberately shot wider. For you must know that much is still preserved of ancient lore among the Rulers of the city that is not spread abroad. We of my house are not of the line of Elendil, though the blood of Númenor is in us. For we reckon back our line to Mardil, the good steward, who ruled in the king's stead when he went away to war. And that was King Eärnur, last of the line of Anárion, and childless, and he came never back. And the stewards have governed the city since that day, though it was many generations of Men ago.

'And this I remember of Boromir as a boy, when we together learned the tale of our sires and the history of our city, that always it displeased him that his father was not king. "How many hundreds of years needs it to make a steward a king, if the king returns not?" he asked. "Few years, maybe, in other places of less royalty," my father answered. "In Gondor ten thousand years would not suffice."

Alas! poor Boromir. Does that not tell you something of him?'

'It does,' said Frodo. 'Yet always he treated Aragorn with honour.'

'I doubt it not,' said Faramir. 'If he were satisfied of Aragorn's claim, as you say, he would greatly reverence him. But the pinch had not yet come. They had not yet reached Minas Tirith or become rivals in her wars.

'But I stray. We in the house of Denethor know much ancient lore by long tradition, and there are moreover in our treasuries many things preserved: books and tablets writ on withered parchments, yea, and on stone, and on leaves of silver and of gold, in divers characters. Some none can now read; and for the rest, few ever unlock them. I can read a little in them, for I have had teaching. It was these records that brought the Grey Pilgrim to us. I first saw him when I was a child, and he has been twice or thrice since then.'

'The Grey Pilgrim?' said Frodo. 'Had he a name?'

'Mithrandir we called him in elf-fashion,' said Faramir, 'and he was content. *Many are my names in many countries,* he said. *Mithrandir among the Elves, Tharkûn to the Dwarves; Olórin I was in my youth in the West that is forgotten, in the South Incánus, in the North Gandalf; to the East I go not.'*

'Gandalf!' said Frodo. 'I thought it was he. Gandalf the Grey, dearest of counsellors. Leader of our Company. He was lost in Moria.'

'Mithrandir was lost!' said Faramir. 'An evil fate seems to have pursued your fellowship. It is hard indeed to believe that one of so great wisdom, and of power – for many wonderful things he did among us – could perish, and so much lore be taken from the world. Are you sure of this, and that he did not just leave you and depart where he would?'

'Alas! yes,' said Frodo. 'I saw him fall into the abyss.'

'I see that there is some great tale of dread in this,' said Faramir, 'which perhaps you may tell me in the evening-time. This Mithrandir was, I now guess, more than a lore-master:

a great mover of the deeds that are done in our time. Had he been among us to consult concerning the hard words of our dream, he could have made them clear to us without need of messenger. Yet, maybe, he would not have done so, and the journey of Boromir was doomed. Mithrandir never spoke to us of what was to be, nor did he reveal his purposes. He got leave of Denethor, how I do not know, to look at the secrets of our treasury, and I learned a little of him, when he would teach (and that was seldom). Ever he would search and would question us above all else concerning the Great Battle that was fought upon Dagorlad in the beginning of Gondor, when He whom we do not name was overthrown. And he was eager for stories of Isildur, though of him we had less to tell; for nothing certain was ever known among us of his end.'

Now Faramir's voice sank to a whisper. 'But this much I learned, or guessed, and I have kept it ever secret in my heart since: that Isildur took somewhat from the hand of the Unnamed, ere he went away from Gondor, never to be seen among mortal men again. Here I thought was the answer to Mithrandir's questioning. But it seemed then a matter that concerned only the seekers after ancient learning. Nor when the riddling words of our dream were debated among us, did I think of *Isildur's Bane* as being this same thing. For Isildur was ambushed and slain by orc-arrows, according to the only legend that we knew, and Mithrandir had never told me more.

'What in truth this Thing is I cannot yet guess; but some heirloom of power and peril it must be. A fell weapon, perchance, devised by the Dark Lord. If it were a thing that gave advantage in battle, I can well believe that Boromir, the proud and fearless, often rash, ever anxious for the victory of Minas Tirith (and his own glory therein), might desire such a thing and be allured by it. Alas that ever he went on that errand! I should have been chosen by my father and the elders, but he put himself forward, as being the older and the hardier (both true), and he would not be stayed.

'But fear no more! I would not take this thing, if it lay by the highway. Not were Minas Tirith falling in ruin and I alone could save her, so, using the weapon of the Dark Lord for her good and my glory. No, I do not wish for such triumphs, Frodo son of Drogo.'

'Neither did the Council,' said Frodo. 'Nor do I. I would have nothing to do with such matters.'

'For myself,' said Faramir, 'I would see the White Tree in flower again in the courts of the kings, and the Silver Crown return, and Minas Tirith in peace: Minas Anor again as of old, full of light, high and fair, beautiful as a queen among other queens: not a mistress of many slaves, nay, not even a kind mistress of willing slaves. War must be, while we defend our lives against a destroyer who would devour all; but I do not love the bright sword for its sharpness, nor the arrow for its swiftness, nor the warrior for his glory. I love only that which they defend: the city of the Men of Númenor; and I would have her loved for her memory, her ancientry, her beauty, and her present wisdom. Not feared, save as men may fear the dignity of a man, old and wise.

'So fear me not! I do not ask you to tell me more. I do not even ask you to tell me whether I now speak nearer the mark. But if you will trust me, it may be that I can advise you in your present quest, whatever that be – yes, and even aid you.'

Frodo made no answer. Almost he yielded to the desire for help and counsel, to tell this grave young man, whose words seemed so wise and fair, all that was in his mind. But something held him back. His heart was heavy with fear and sorrow: if he and Sam were indeed, as seemed likely, all that was now left of the Nine Walkers, then he was in sole command of the secret of their errand. Better mistrust undeserved than rash words. And the memory of Boromir, of the dreadful change that the lure of the Ring had worked in him, was very present to his mind, when he looked at Faramir and listened to his voice: unlike they were, and yet also much akin.

*   *   *

They walked on in silence for a while, passing like grey and green shadows under the old trees, their feet making no sound; above them many birds sang, and the sun glistened on the polished roof of dark leaves in the evergreen woods of Ithilien.

Sam had taken no part in the conversation, though he had listened; and at the same time he had attended with his keen hobbit ears to all the soft woodland noises about them. One thing he had noted, that in all the talk the name of Gollum had not once come up. He was glad, though he felt that it was too much to hope that he would never hear it again. He soon became aware also that though they walked alone, there were many men close at hand: not only Damrod and Mablung flitting in and out of the shadows ahead, but others on either side, all making their swift secret way to some appointed place.

Once, looking suddenly back, as if some prickle of the skin told him that he was watched from behind, he thought he caught a brief glimpse of a small dark shape slipping behind a tree-trunk. He opened his mouth to speak and shut it again. 'I'm not sure of it,' he said to himself, 'and why should I remind them of the old villain, if they choose to forget him? I wish I could!'

So they passed on, until the woodlands grew thinner and the land began to fall more steeply. Then they turned aside again, to the right, and came quickly to a small river in a narrow gorge: it was the same stream that trickled far above out of the round pool, now grown to a swift torrent, leaping down over many stones in a deep-cloven bed, overhung with ilex and dark box-woods. Looking west they could see, below them in a haze of light, lowlands and broad meads, and glinting far off in the westering sun the wide waters of the Anduin.

'Here, alas! I must do you a discourtesy,' said Faramir. 'I hope you will pardon it to one who has so far made his orders give way to courtesy as not to slay you or to bind you. But it is a command that no stranger, not even one of Rohan that fights with us, shall see the path we now go with open eyes. I must blindfold you.'

'As you will,' said Frodo. 'Even the Elves do likewise at need, and blindfolded we crossed the borders of fair Loth-lórien. Gimli the dwarf took it ill, but the hobbits endured it.'

'It is to no place so fair that I shall lead you,' said Faramir. 'But I am glad that you will take this willingly and not by force.'

He called softly and immediately Mablung and Damrod stepped out of the trees and came back to him. 'Blindfold these guests,' said Faramir. 'Securely, but not so as to dis-comfort them. Do not tie their hands. They will give their word not to try and see. I could trust them to shut their eyes of their own accord, but eyes will blink, if the feet stumble. Lead them so that they do not falter.'

With green scarves the two guards now bound up the hobbits' eyes, and drew their hoods down almost to their mouths; then quickly they took each one by the hand and went on their way. All that Frodo and Sam knew of this last mile of the road they learned from guessing in the dark. After a little they found that they were on a path descending steeply; soon it grew so narrow that they went in single file, brushing a stony wall on either side; their guards steered them from behind with hands laid firmly on their shoulders. Now and again they came to rough places and were lifted from their feet for a while, and then set down again. Always the noise of the running water was on their right hand, and it grew nearer and louder. At length they were halted. Quickly Mab-lung and Damrod turned them about, several times, and they lost all sense of direction. They climbed upwards a little: it seemed cold and the noise of the stream had become faint. Then they were picked up and carried down, down many steps, and round a corner. Suddenly they heard the water again, loud now, rushing and splashing. All round them it seemed, and they felt a fine rain on their hands and cheeks. At last they were set on their feet once more. For a moment they stood so, half fearful, blindfold, not knowing where they were; and no one spoke.

Then came the voice of Faramir close behind. 'Let them see!' he said. The scarves were removed and their hoods drawn back, and they blinked and gasped.

They stood on a wet floor of polished stone, the doorstep, as it were, of a rough-hewn gate of rock opening dark behind them. But in front a thin veil of water was hung, so near that Frodo could have put an outstretched arm into it. It faced westward. The level shafts of the setting sun behind beat upon it, and the red light was broken into many flickering beams of ever-changing colour. It was as if they stood at the window of some elven-tower, curtained with threaded jewels of silver and gold, and ruby, sapphire and amethyst, all kindled with an unconsuming fire.

'At least by good chance we came at the right hour to reward you for your patience,' said Faramir. 'This is the Window of the Sunset, Henneth Annûn, fairest of all the falls of Ithilien, land of many fountains. Few strangers have ever seen it. But there is no kingly hall behind to match it. Enter now and see!'

Even as he spoke the sun sank, and the fire faded in the flowing water. They turned and passed under the low forbidding arch. At once they found themselves in a rock-chamber, wide and rough, with an uneven stooping roof. A few torches were kindled and cast a dim light on the glistening walls. Many men were already there. Others were still coming in by twos and threes through a dark narrow door on one side. As their eyes grew accustomed to the gloom the hobbits saw that the cave was larger than they had guessed and was filled with great store of arms and victuals.

'Well, here is our refuge,' said Faramir. 'Not a place of great ease, but here you may pass the night in peace. It is dry at least, and there is food, though no fire. At one time the water flowed down through this cave and out of the arch, but its course was changed further up the gorge, by workmen of old, and the stream sent down in a fall of doubled height over the rocks far above. All the ways into this grot were then sealed against the entry of water or aught else, all save one. There are now but two ways out: that passage yonder by which you entered blindfold, and through the Window-curtain into a deep bowl filled with knives of stone. Now rest a while, until the evening meal is set.'

The hobbits were taken to a corner and given a low bed to lie on, if they wished. Meanwhile men busied themselves about the cave, quietly and in orderly quickness. Light tables were taken from the walls and set up on trestles and laden with gear. This was plain and unadorned for the most part, but all well and fairly made: round platters, bowls and dishes of glazed brown clay or turned box-wood, smooth and clean. Here and there was a cup or basin of polished bronze; and a goblet of plain silver was set by the Captain's seat in the middle of the inmost table.

Faramir went about among the men, questioning each as he came in, in a soft voice. Some came back from the pursuit of the Southrons; others, left behind as scouts near the road, came in latest. All the Southrons had been accounted for, save only the great mûmak: what happened to him none could say. Of the enemy no movement could be seen; not even an orc-spy was abroad.

'You saw and heard nothing, Anborn?' Faramir asked of the latest comer.

'Well, no, lord,' said the man. 'No Orc at least. But I saw, or thought I saw, something a little strange. It was getting deep dusk, when the eyes make things greater than they should be. So perhaps it may have been no more than a squirrel.' Sam pricked up his ears at this. 'Yet if so, it was a black squirrel, and I saw no tail. 'Twas like a shadow on the ground, and it whisked behind a tree-trunk when I drew nigh and went up aloft as swift as any squirrel could. You will not have us slay wild beasts for no purpose, and it seemed no more, so I tried no arrow. It was too dark for sure shooting anyway, and the creature was gone into the gloom of the leaves in a twinkling. But I stayed for a while, for it seemed strange, and then I hastened back. I thought I heard the thing hiss at me from high above as I turned away. A large squirrel, maybe. Perhaps under the shadow of the Unnamed some of the beasts of Mirkwood are wandering hither to our woods. They have black squirrels there, 'tis said.'

'Perhaps,' said Faramir. 'But that would be an ill omen, if it were so. We do not want the escapes of Mirkwood in Ithilien.' Sam fancied that he gave a swift glance towards the hobbits as he spoke; but Sam said nothing. For a while he and Frodo lay back and watched the torchlight, and the men moving to and fro speaking in hushed voices. Then suddenly Frodo fell asleep.

Sam struggled with himself, arguing this way and that. 'He may be all right,' he thought, 'and then he may not. Fair speech may hide a foul heart.' He yawned. 'I could sleep for a week, and I'd be better for it. And what can I do, if I do keep awake, me all alone, and all these great Men about? Nothing, Sam Gamgee; but you've got to keep awake all the same.' And somehow he managed it. The light faded from the cave door, and the grey veil of falling water grew dim and was lost in gathering shadow. Always the sound of the water went on, never changing its note, morning or evening or night. It murmured and whispered of sleep. Sam stuck his knuckles in his eyes.

Now more torches were being lit. A cask of wine was broached. Storage barrels were being opened. Men were fetching water from the fall. Some were laving their hands in basins. A wide copper bowl and a white cloth were brought to Faramir and he washed.

'Wake our guests,' he said, 'and take them water. It is time to eat.'

Frodo sat up and yawned and stretched. Sam, not used to being waited on, looked with some surprise at the tall man who bowed, holding a basin of water before him.

'Put it on the ground, master, if you please!' he said. 'Easier for me and you.' Then to the astonishment and amusement of the Men he plunged his head into the cold water and splashed his neck and ears.

'Is it the custom in your land to wash the head before supper?' said the man who waited on the hobbits.

'No, before breakfast,' said Sam. 'But if you're short of sleep cold water on the neck's like rain on a wilted lettuce. There! Now I can keep awake long enough to eat a bit.'

They were led then to seats beside Faramir: barrels covered with pelts and high enough above the benches of the Men for their convenience. Before they ate, Faramir and all his men turned and faced west in a moment of silence. Faramir signed to Frodo and Sam that they should do likewise.

'So we always do,' he said, as they sat down: 'we look towards Númenor that was, and beyond to Elvenhome that is, and to that which is beyond Elvenhome and will ever be. Have you no such custom at meat?'

'No,' said Frodo, feeling strangely rustic and untutored. 'But if we are guests, we bow to our host, and after we have eaten we rise and thank him.'

'That we do also,' said Faramir.

After so long journeying and camping, and days spent in the lonely wild, the evening meal seemed a feast to the hobbits: to drink pale yellow wine, cool and fragrant, and eat bread and butter, and salted meats, and dried fruits, and good red cheese, with clean hands and clean knives and plates. Neither Frodo nor Sam refused anything that was offered, nor a second, nor indeed a third helping. The wine coursed in their veins and tired limbs, and they felt glad and easy of heart as they had not done since they left the land of Lórien.

When all was done Faramir led them to a recess at the back of the cave, partly screened by curtains; and a chair and two stools were brought there. A little earthenware lamp burned in a niche.

'You may soon desire to sleep,' he said, 'and especially

good Samwise, who would not close his eyes before he ate – whether for fear of blunting the edge of a noble hunger, or for fear of me, I do not know. But it is not good to sleep too soon after meat, and that following a fast. Let us talk a while. On your journey from Rivendell there must have been many things to tell. And you, too, would perhaps wish to learn something of us and the lands where you now are. Tell me of Boromir my brother, and of old Mithrandir, and of the fair people of Lothlórien.'

Frodo no longer felt sleepy and he was willing to talk. But though the food and wine had put him at his ease, he had not lost all his caution. Sam was beaming and humming to himself, but when Frodo spoke he was at first content to listen, only occasionally venturing to make an exclamation of agreement.

Frodo told many tales, yet always he steered the matter away from the quest of the Company and from the Ring, enlarging rather on the valiant part Boromir had played in all their adventures, with the wolves of the wild, in the snows under Caradhras, and in the mines of Moria where Gandalf fell. Faramir was most moved by the story of the fight on the bridge.

'It must have irked Boromir to run from Orcs,' he said, 'or even from the fell thing you name, the Balrog – even though he was the last to leave.'

'He was the last,' said Frodo, 'but Aragorn was forced to lead us. He alone knew the way after Gandalf's fall. But had there not been us lesser folk to care for, I do not think that either he or Boromir would have fled.'

'Maybe, it would have been better had Boromir fallen there with Mithrandir,' said Faramir, 'and not gone on to the fate that waited above the falls of Rauros.'

'Maybe. But tell me now of your own fortunes,' said Frodo, turning the matter aside once again. 'For I would learn more of Minas Ithil and Osgiliath, and Minas Tirith the long-enduring. What hope have you for that city in your long war?'

'What hope have we?' said Faramir. 'It is long since we had any hope. The sword of Elendil, if it returns indeed, may rekindle it, but I do not think that it will do more than put off the evil day, unless other help unlooked-for also comes, from Elves or Men. For the Enemy increases and we decrease. We are a failing people, a springless autumn.

'The Men of Númenor were settled far and wide on the shores and seaward regions of the Great Lands, but for the most part they fell into evils and follies. Many became enamoured of the Darkness and the black arts; some were given over wholly to idleness and ease, and some fought among themselves, until they were conquered in their weakness by the wild men.

'It is not said that evil arts were ever practised in Gondor, or that the Nameless One was ever named in honour there; and the old wisdom and beauty brought out of the West remained long in the realm of the sons of Elendil the Fair, and they linger there still. Yet even so it was Gondor that brought about its own decay, falling by degrees into dotage, and thinking that the Enemy was asleep, who was only banished not destroyed.

'Death was ever present, because the Númenoreans still, as they had in their old kingdom, and so lost it, hungered after endless life unchanging. Kings made tombs more splendid than houses of the living, and counted old names in the rolls of their descent dearer than the names of sons. Childless lords sat in aged halls musing on heraldry; in secret chambers withered men compounded strong elixirs, or in high cold towers asked questions of the stars. And the last king of the line of Anárion had no heir.

'But the stewards were wiser and more fortunate. Wiser, for they recruited the strength of our people from the sturdy folk of the sea-coast, and from the hardy mountaineers of Ered Nimrais. And they made a truce with the proud peoples of the North, who often had assailed us, men of fierce valour, but our kin from afar off, unlike the wild Easterlings or the cruel Haradrim.

'So it came to pass in the days of Cirion the Twelfth Steward (and my father is the six and twentieth) that they rode to our aid and at the great Field of Celebrant they destroyed our enemies that had seized our northern provinces. These are the Rohirrim, as we name them, masters of horses, and we ceded to them the fields of Calenardhon that are since called Rohan; for that province had long been sparsely peopled. And they became our allies, and have ever proved true to us, aiding us at need, and guarding our northern marches and the Gap of Rohan.

'Of our lore and manners they have learned what they would, and their lords speak our speech at need; yet for the most part they hold by the ways of their own fathers and to their own memories, and they speak among themselves their own North tongue. And we love them: tall men and fair women, valiant both alike, golden-haired, bright-eyed, and strong; they remind us of the youth of Men, as they were in the Elder Days. Indeed it is said by our lore-masters that they have from of old this affinity with us that they are come from those same Three Houses of Men as were the Númenoreans in their beginning; not from Hador the Goldenhaired, the Elf-friend, maybe, yet from such of his sons and people as went not over Sea into the West, refusing the call.

'For so we reckon Men in our lore, calling them the High, or Men of the West, which were Númenoreans; and the Middle Peoples, Men of the Twilight, such as are the Rohirrim and their kin that dwell still far in the North; and the Wild, the Men of Darkness.

'Yet now, if the Rohirrim are grown in some ways more like to us, enhanced in arts and gentleness, we too have become more like to them, and can scarce claim any longer the title High. We are become Middle Men, of the Twilight, but with memory of other things. For as the Rohirrim do, we now love war and valour as things good in themselves, both a sport and an end; and though we still hold that a warrior should have more skills and knowledge than only the craft of weapons and slaying, we esteem a warrior, nonetheless, above men of other crafts. Such is the need of our days. So even was my brother, Boromir: a man of prowess, and for that he was accounted the best man in Gondor. And very valiant indeed he was: no heir of Minas Tirith has for long years been so hardy in toil, so onward into battle, or blown a mightier note on the Great Horn.' Faramir sighed and fell silent for a while.

'You don't say much in all your tales about the Elves, sir,' said Sam, suddenly plucking up courage. He had noted that Faramir seemed to refer to Elves with reverence, and this even more than his courtesy, and his food and wine, had won Sam's respect and quieted his suspicions.

'No indeed, Master Samwise,' said Faramir, 'for I am not learned in Elven-lore. But there you touch upon another point in which we have changed, declining from Númenor to Middle-earth. For as you may know, if Mithrandir was your companion and you have spoken with Elrond, the Edain, the Fathers of the Númenoreans, fought beside the Elves in the first wars, and were rewarded by the gift of the kingdom in the midst of the Sea, within sight of Elven-home. But in Middle-earth Men and Elves became estranged in the days of darkness, by the arts of the Enemy, and by the slow changes of time in which each kind walked further down their sundered roads. Men now fear and misdoubt the Elves, and yet know little of them. And we of Gondor grow like other Men, like the men of Rohan; for even they, who are foes of the Dark Lord, shun the Elves and speak of the Golden Wood with dread.

'Yet there are among us still some who have dealings with the Elves when they may, and ever and anon one will go in secret to Lórien, seldom to return. Not I. For I deem it perilous now for mortal man wilfully to seek out the Elder People. Yet I envy you that have spoken with the White Lady.'

'The Lady of Lórien! Galadriel!' cried Sam. 'You should

see her, indeed you should, sir. I am only a hobbit, and gardening's my job at home, sir, if you understand me, and I'm not much good at poetry – not at making it: a bit of a comic rhyme, perhaps, now and again, you know, but not real poetry – so I can't tell you what I mean. It ought to be sung. You'd have to get Strider, Aragorn that is, or old Mr. Bilbo, for that. But I wish I could make a song about her. Beautiful she is, sir! Lovely! Sometimes like a great tree in flower, sometimes like a white daffadowndilly, small and slender like. Hard as di'monds, soft as moonlight. Warm as sunlight, cold as frost in the stars. Proud and far-off as a snow-mountain, and as merry as any lass I ever saw with daisies in her hair in springtime. But that's a lot o' nonsense, and all wide of my mark.'

'Then she must be lovely indeed,' said Faramir. 'Perilously fair.'

'I don't know about *perilous*,' said Sam. 'It strikes me that folk takes their peril with them into Lórien, and finds it there because they've brought it. But perhaps you could call her perilous, because she's so strong in herself. You, you could dash yourself to pieces on her, like a ship on a rock; or drownd yourself, like a hobbit in a river. But neither rock nor river would be to blame. Now Boro———' He stopped and went red in the face.

'Yes? *Now Boromir* you would say?' said Faramir. 'What would you say? He took his peril with him?'

'Yes sir, begging your pardon, and a fine man as your brother was, if I may say so. But you've been warm on the scent all along. Now I watched Boromir and listened to him, from Rivendell all down the road – looking after my master, as you'll understand, and not meaning any harm to Boromir – and it's my opinion that in Lórien he first saw clearly what I guessed sooner: what he wanted. From the moment he first saw it he wanted the Enemy's Ring!'

'Sam!' cried Frodo aghast. He had fallen deep into his own thoughts for a while, and came out of them suddenly and too late.

'Save me!' said Sam turning white, and then flushing scarlet. 'There I go again! *When ever you open your big mouth you
put your foot in it* the Gaffer used to say to me, and right
enough. O dear, O dear!

'Now look here, sir!' He turned, facing up to Faramir with
all the courage that he could muster. 'Don't you go taking
advantage of my master because his servant's no better than
a fool. You've spoken very handsome all along, put me off
my guard, talking of Elves and all. But *handsome is as handsome does* we say. Now's a chance to show your quality.'

'So it seems,' said Faramir, slowly and very softly, with a
strange smile. 'So that is the answer to all the riddles! The
One Ring that was thought to have perished from the world.
And Boromir tried to take it by force? And you escaped?
And ran all the way – to me! And here in the wild I have
you: two halflings, and a host of men at my call, and the
Ring of Rings. A pretty stroke of fortune! A chance for Faramir, Captain of Gondor, to show his quality! Ha!' He stood
up, very tall and stern, his grey eyes glinting.

Frodo and Sam sprang from their stools and set themselves
side by side with their backs to the wall, fumbling for their
sword-hilts. There was a silence. All the men in the cave
stopped talking and looked towards them in wonder. But
Faramir sat down again in his chair and began to laugh
quietly, and then suddenly became grave again.

'Alas for Boromir! It was too sore a trial!' he said. 'How
you have increased my sorrow, you two strange wanderers
from a far country, bearing the peril of Men! But you are
less judges of Men than I of Halflings. We are truth-speakers,
we men of Gondor. We boast seldom, and then perform, or
die in the attempt. *Not if I found it on the highway would I
take it* I said. Even if I were such a man as to desire this
thing, and even though I knew not clearly what this thing
was when I spoke, still I should take those words as a vow,
and be held by them.

'But I am not such a man. Or I am wise enough to know
that there are some perils from which a man must flee. Sit

at peace! And be comforted, Samwise. If you seem to have stumbled, think that it was fated to be so. Your heart is shrewd as well as faithful, and saw clearer than your eyes. For strange though it may seem, it was safe to declare this to me. It may even help the master that you love. It shall turn to his good, if it is in my power. So be comforted. But do not even name this thing again aloud. Once is enough.'

The hobbits came back to their seats and sat very quiet. Men turned back to their drink and their talk, perceiving that their captain had had some jest or other with the little guests, and that it was over.

'Well, Frodo, now at last we understand one another,' said Faramir. 'If you took this thing on yourself, unwilling, at others' asking, then you have pity and honour from me. And I marvel at you: to keep it hid and not to use it. You are a new people and a new world to me. Are all your kin of like sort? Your land must be a realm of peace and content, and there must gardeners be in high honour.'

'Not all is well there,' said Frodo, 'but certainly gardeners are honoured.'

'But folk must grow weary there, even in their gardens, as do all things under the Sun of this world. And you are far from home and wayworn. No more tonight. Sleep, both of you – in peace, if you can. Fear not! I do not wish to see it, or touch it, or know more of it than I know (which is enough), lest peril perchance waylay me and I fall lower in the test than Frodo son of Drogo. Go now to rest – but first tell me only, if you will, whither you wish to go, and what to do. For I must watch, and wait, and think. Time passes. In the morning we must each go swiftly on the ways appointed to us.'

Frodo had felt himself trembling as the first shock of fear passed. Now a great weariness came down on him like a cloud. He could dissemble and resist no longer.

'I was going to find a way into Mordor,' he said faintly. 'I was going to Gorgoroth. I must find the Mountain of Fire and cast the thing into the gulf of Doom. Gandalf said so. I do not think I shall ever get there.'

Faramir stared at him for a moment in grave astonishment. Then suddenly he caught him as he swayed, and lifting him gently, carried him to the bed and laid him there, and covered him warmly. At once he fell into a deep sleep.

Another bed was set beside him for his servant. Sam hesitated for a moment, then bowing very low: 'Good night, Captain, my lord,' he said. 'You took the chance, sir.'

'Did I so?' said Faramir.

'Yes sir, and showed your quality: the very highest.'

Faramir smiled. 'A pert servant, Master Samwise. But nay: the praise of the praiseworthy is above all rewards. Yet there was naught in this to praise. I had no lure or desire to do other than I have done.'

'Ah well, sir,' said Sam, 'you said my master had an elvish air; and that was good and true. But I can say this: you have an air too, sir, that reminds me of, of – well, Gandalf, of wizards.'

'Maybe,' said Faramir. 'Maybe you discern from far away the air of Númenor. Good night!'

CHAPTER VI

THE FORBIDDEN POOL

Frodo woke to find Faramir bending over him. For a second old fears seized him and he sat up and shrank away.

'There is nothing to fear,' said Faramir.

'Is it morning already?' said Frodo yawning.

'Not yet, but night is drawing to an end, and the full moon is setting. Will you come and see it? Also there is a matter on which I desire your counsel. I am sorry to rouse you from sleep, but will you come?'

'I will,' said Frodo, rising and shivering a little as he left the warm blanket and pelts. It seemed cold in the fireless cave. The noise of the water was loud in the stillness. He put on his cloak and followed Faramir.

Sam, waking suddenly by some instinct of watchfulness, saw first his master's empty bed and leapt to his feet. Then he saw two dark figures, Frodo and a man, framed against the archway, which was now filled with a pale white light. He hurried after them, past rows of men sleeping on mattresses along the wall. As he went by the cave-mouth he saw that the Curtain was now become a dazzling veil of silk and pearls and silver thread: melting icicles of moonlight. But he did not pause to admire it, and turning aside he followed his master through the narrow doorway in the wall of the cave.

They went first along a black passage, then up many wet steps, and so came to a small flat landing cut in the stone and lit by the pale sky, gleaming high above through a long deep shaft. From here two flights of steps led: one going on, as it seemed, up on to the high bank of the stream; the other turning away to the left. This they followed. It wound its way up like a turret-stair.

*   *   *

At last they came out of the stony darkness and looked about. They were on a wide flat rock without rail or parapet. At their right, eastwards, the torrent fell, splashing over many terraces, and then, pouring down a steep race, it filled a smooth-hewn channel with a dark force of water flecked with foam, and curling and rushing almost at their feet it plunged sheer over the edge that yawned upon their left. A man stood there, near the brink, silent, gazing down.

Frodo turned to watch the sleek necks of the water as they curved and dived. Then he lifted his eyes and gazed far away. The world was quiet and cold, as if dawn were near. Far off in the West the full moon was sinking, round and white. Pale mists shimmered in the great vale below: a wide gulf of silver fume, beneath which rolled the cool night-waters of the Anduin. A black darkness loomed beyond, and in it glinted, here and there, cold, sharp, remote, white as the teeth of ghosts, the peaks of Ered Nimrais, the White Mountains of the realm of Gondor, tipped with everlasting snow.

For a while Frodo stood there on the high stone, and a shiver ran through him, wondering if anywhere in the vastness of the nightlands his old companions walked or slept, or lay dead shrouded in mist. Why was he brought here out of forgetful sleep?

Sam was eager for an answer to the same question and could not refrain himself from muttering, for his master's ear alone as he thought: 'It's a fine view, no doubt, Mr. Frodo, but chilly to the heart, not to mention the bones! What's going on?'

Faramir heard and answered. 'Moonset over Gondor. Fair Ithil, as he goes from Middle-earth, glances upon the white locks of old Mindolluin. It is worth a few shivers. But that is not what I brought you to see – though as for you, Samwise, you were not brought, and do but pay the penalty of your watchfulness. A draught of wine shall amend it. Come, look now!'

He stepped up beside the silent sentinel on the dark edge, and Frodo followed. Sam hung back. He already felt insecure enough on this high wet platform. Faramir and Frodo looked down. Far below them they saw the white waters pour into a foaming bowl, and then swirl darkly about a deep oval basin in the rocks, until they found their way out again through a narrow gate, and flowed away, fuming and chattering, into calmer and more level reaches. The moonlight still slanted down to the fall's foot and gleamed on the ripples of the basin. Presently Frodo was aware of a small dark thing on the near bank, but even as he looked at it, it dived and vanished just beyond the boil and bubble of the fall, cleaving the black water as neatly as an arrow or an edgewise stone.

Faramir turned to the man at his side. 'Now what would you say that it is, Anborn? A squirrel, or a kingfisher? Are there black kingfishers in the night-pools of Mirkwood?'

''Tis not a bird, whatever else it be,' answered Anborn. 'It has four limbs and dives manwise; a pretty mastery of the craft it shows, too. What is it at? Seeking a way up behind the Curtain to our hidings? It seems we are discovered at last. I have my bow here, and I have posted other archers, nigh as good marksmen as myself, on either bank. We wait only for your command to shoot, Captain.'

'Shall we shoot?' said Faramir, turning quickly to Frodo.

Frodo did not answer for a moment. Then 'No!' he said. 'No! I beg you not to.' If Sam had dared, he would have said 'Yes,' quicker and louder. He could not see, but he guessed well enough from their words what they were looking at.

'You know, then, what this thing is?' said Faramir. 'Come, now you have seen, tell me why it should be spared. In all our words together you have not once spoken of your gangrel companion, and I let him be for the time. He could wait till he was caught and brought before me. I sent my keenest huntsmen to seek him, but he slipped them, and they had no sight of him till now, save Anborn here, once at dusk yesterevening. But now he has done worse trespass than only to go coney-snaring in the uplands: he has dared to come to Henneth Annûn, and his life is forfeit. I marvel at the creature: so secret and so sly as he is, to come sporting in the

pool before our very window. Does he think that men sleep
without watch all night? Why does he so?'

'There are two answers, I think,' said Frodo. 'For one
thing, he knows little of Men, and sly though he is, your
refuge is so hidden that perhaps he does not know that Men
are concealed here. For another, I think he is allured here by
a mastering desire, stronger than his caution.'

'He is lured here, you say?' said Faramir in a low voice.
'Can he, does he then know of your burden?'

'Indeed yes. He bore it himself for many years.'

'*He* bore it?' said Faramir, breathing sharply in his wonder.
'This matter winds itself ever in new riddles. Then he is
pursuing it?'

'Maybe. It is precious to him. But I did not speak of that.'

'What then does the creature seek?'

'Fish,' said Frodo. 'Look!'

They peered down at the dark pool. A little black head
appeared at the far end of the basin, just out of the deep
shadow of the rocks. There was a brief silver glint, and a
swirl of tiny ripples. It swam to the side, and then with marvellous agility a froglike figure climbed out of the water and
up the bank. At once it sat down and began to gnaw at the
small silver thing that glittered as it turned: the last rays of
the moon were now falling behind the stony wall at the pool's
end.

Faramir laughed softly. 'Fish!' he said. 'It is a less perilous
hunger. Or maybe not: fish from the pool of Henneth Annûn
may cost him all he has to give.'

'Now I have him at the arrow-point,' said Anborn. 'Shall
I not shoot, Captain? For coming unbidden to this place
death is our law.'

'Wait, Anborn,' said Faramir. 'This is a harder matter than
it seems. What have you to say now, Frodo? Why should we
spare?'

'The creature is wretched and hungry,' said Frodo, 'and
unaware of his danger. And Gandalf, your Mithrandir, he

would have bidden you not to slay him for that reason, and for others. He forbade the Elves to do so. I do not know clearly why, and of what I guess I cannot speak openly out here. But this creature is in some way bound up with my errand. Until you found us and took us, he was my guide.'

'Your guide!' said Faramir. 'The matter becomes ever stranger. I would do much for you, Frodo, but this I cannot grant: to let this sly wanderer go free at his own will from here, to join you later if it please him, or to be caught by orcs and tell all he knows under threat of pain. He must be slain or taken. Slain, if he be not taken very swiftly. But how can this slippery thing of many guises be caught, save by a feathered shaft?'

'Let me go down quietly to him,' said Frodo. 'You may keep your bows bent, and shoot me at least, if I fail. I shall not run away.'

'Go then and be swift!' said Faramir. 'If he comes off alive, he should be your faithful servant for the rest of his unhappy days. Lead Frodo down to the bank, Anborn, and go softly. The thing has a nose and ears. Give me your bow.'

Anborn grunted and led the way down the winding stair to the landing, and then up the other stair, until at last they came to a narrow opening shrouded with thick bushes. Passing silently through, Frodo found himself on the top of the southern bank above the pool. It was now dark and the falls were pale and grey, reflecting only the lingering moonlight of the western sky. He could not see Gollum. He went forward a short way and Anborn came softly behind him.

'Go on!' he breathed in Frodo's ear. 'Have a care to your right. If you fall in the pool, then no one but your fishing friend can help you. And forget not that there are bowmen near at hand, though you may not see them.'

Frodo crept forward, using his hands Gollum-like to feel his way and to steady himself. The rocks were for the most part flat and smooth but slippery. He halted listening. At first he could hear no sound but the unceasing rush of the fall behind him. Then presently he heard, not far ahead, a hissing murmur.

'Fissh, nice fissh. White Face has vanished, my precious, at last, yes. Now we can eat fish in peace. No, not in peace, precious. For Precious is lost; yes, lost. Dirty hobbits, nasty hobbits. Gone and left us, *gollum*; and Precious is gone. Only poor Sméagol all alone. No Precious. Nasty Men, they'll take it, steal my Precious. Thieves. We hates them. Fissh, nice fissh. Makes us strong. Makes eyes bright, fingers tight, yes. Throttle them, precious. Throttle them all, yes, if we gets chances. Nice fissh. Nice fissh!'

So it went on, almost as unceasing as the waterfall, only interrupted by a faint noise of slavering and gurgling. Frodo shivered, listening with pity and disgust. He wished it would stop, and that he never need hear that voice again. Anborn was not far behind. He could creep back and ask him to get the huntsmen to shoot. They would probably get close enough, while Gollum was gorging and off his guard. Only one true shot, and Frodo would be rid of the miserable voice for ever. But no, Gollum had a claim on him now. The servant has a claim on the master for service, even service in fear. They would have foundered in the Dead Marshes but for Gollum. Frodo knew, too, somehow, quite clearly that Gandalf would not have wished it.

'Sméagol!' he said softly.

'Fissh, nice fissh,' said the voice.

'Sméagol!' he said, a little louder. The voice stopped.

'Sméagol, Master has come to look for you. Master is here. Come, Sméagol!' There was no answer but a soft hiss, as of intaken breath.

'Come, Sméagol!' said Frodo. 'We are in danger. Men will kill you, if they find you here. Come quickly, if you wish to escape death. Come to Master!'

'No!' said the voice. 'Not nice Master. Leaves poor Sméagol and goes with new friends. Master can wait. Sméagol hasn't finished.'

'There's no time,' said Frodo. 'Bring fish with you. Come!'

'No! Must finish fish.'

'Sméagol!' said Frodo desperately. 'Precious will be angry. I shall take Precious, and I shall say: make him swallow the bones and choke. Never taste fish again. Come, Precious is waiting!'

There was a sharp hiss. Presently out of the darkness Gollum came crawling on all fours, like an erring dog called to heel. He had a half-eaten fish in his mouth and another in his hand. He came close to Frodo, almost nose to nose, and sniffed at him. His pale eyes were shining. Then he took the fish out of his mouth and stood up.

'Nice Master!' he whispered. 'Nice hobbit, come back to poor Sméagol. Good Sméagol comes. Now let's go, go quickly, yes. Through the trees, while the Faces are dark. Yes, come, let's go!'

'Yes, we'll go soon,' said Frodo. 'But not at once. I will go with you as I promised. I promise again. But not now. You are not safe yet. I will save you, but you must trust me.'

'We must trust Master?' said Gollum doubtfully. 'Why? Why not go at once? Where is the other one, the cross rude hobbit? Where is he?'

'Away up there,' said Frodo, pointing to the waterfall. 'I am not going without him. We must go back to him.' His heart sank. This was too much like trickery. He did not really fear that Faramir would allow Gollum to be killed, but he would probably make him prisoner and bind him; and certainly what Frodo did would seem a treachery to the poor treacherous creature. It would probably be impossible ever to make him understand or believe that Frodo had saved his life in the only way he could. What else could he do? – to keep faith, as near as might be, with both sides. 'Come!' he said. 'Or the Precious will be angry. We are going back now, up the stream. Go on, go on, you go in front!'

Gollum crawled along close to the brink for a little way, snuffling and suspicious. Presently he stopped and raised his head. 'Something's there!' he said. 'Not a hobbit.' Suddenly he turned back. A green light was flickering in his bulging eyes. 'Masster, masster!' he hissed. 'Wicked! Tricksy! False!' He spat and stretched out his long arms with white snapping fingers.

At that moment the great black shape of Anborn loomed up behind him and came down on him. A large strong hand took him in the nape of the neck and pinned him. He twisted round like lightning, all wet and slimy as he was, wriggling like an eel, biting and scratching like a cat. But two more men came up out of the shadows.

'Hold still!' said one. 'Or we'll stick you as full of pins as a hedgehog. Hold still!'

Gollum went limp, and began to whine and weep. They tied him, none too gently.

'Easy, easy!' said Frodo. 'He has no strength to match you. Don't hurt him, if you can help it. He'll be quieter, if you don't. Sméagol! They won't hurt you. I'll go with you, and you shall come to no harm. Not unless they kill me too. Trust Master!'

Gollum turned and spat at him. The men picked him up, put a hood over his eyes, and carried him off.

Frodo followed them, feeling very wretched. They went through the opening behind the bushes, and back, down the stairs and passages, into the cave. Two or three torches had been lit. Men were stirring. Sam was there, and he gave a queer look at the limp bundle that the men carried. 'Got him?' he said to Frodo.

'Yes. Well no, I didn't get him. He came to me, because he trusted me at first, I'm afraid. I did not want him tied up like this. I hope it will be all right; but I hate the whole business.'

'So do I,' said Sam. 'And nothing will ever be all right where that piece of misery is.'

A man came and beckoned to the hobbits, and took them to the recess at the back of the cave. Faramir was sitting there in his chair, and the lamp had been rekindled in its niche above his head. He signed to them to sit down on the stools beside him. 'Bring wine for the guests,' he said. 'And bring the prisoner to me.'

The wine was brought, and then Anborn came carrying Gollum. He removed the cover from Gollum's head and set him on his feet, standing behind him to support him. Gollum blinked, hooding the malice of his eyes with their heavy pale lids. A very miserable creature he looked, dripping and dank, smelling of fish (he still clutched one in his hand); his sparse locks were hanging like rank weed over his bony brows, his nose was snivelling.

'Loose us! Loose us!' he said. 'The cord hurts us, yes it does, it hurts us, and we've done nothing.'

'Nothing?' said Faramir, looking at the wretched creature with a keen glance, but without any expression in his face either of anger, or pity, or wonder. 'Nothing? Have you never done anything worthy of binding or of worse punishment? However, that is not for me to judge, happily. But tonight you have come where it is death to come. The fish of this pool are dearly bought.'

Gollum dropped the fish from his hand. 'Don't want fish,' he said.

'The price is not set on the fish,' said Faramir. 'Only to come here and look on the pool bears the penalty of death. I have spared you so far at the prayer of Frodo here, who says that of him at least you have deserved some thanks. But you must also satisfy me. What is your name? Whence do you come? And whither do you go? What is your business?'

'We are lost, lost,' said Gollum. 'No name, no business, no Precious, nothing. Only empty. Only hungry; yes, we are hungry. A few little fishes, nasty bony little fishes, for a poor creature, and they say death. So wise they are; so just, so very just.'

'Not very wise,' said Faramir. 'But just: yes perhaps, as just as our little wisdom allows. Unloose him Frodo!' Faramir took a small nail-knife from his belt and handed it to Frodo. Gollum misunderstanding the gesture, squealed and fell down.

'Now, Sméagol!' said Frodo. 'You must trust me. I will
not desert you. Answer truthfully, if you can. It will do you
good not harm.' He cut the cords on Gollum's wrists and
ankles and raised him to his feet.

'Come hither!' said Faramir. 'Look at me! Do you know
the name of this place? Have you been here before?'

Slowly Gollum raised his eyes and looked unwillingly into
Faramir's. All light went out of them, and they stared bleak
and pale for a moment into the clear unwavering eyes of the
man of Gondor. There was a still silence. Then Gollum
dropped his head and shrank down, until he was squatting
on the floor, shivering. 'We doesn't know and we doesn't
want to know,' he whimpered. 'Never came here; never come
again.'

'There are locked doors and closed windows in your mind,
and dark rooms behind them,' said Faramir. 'But in this I
judge that you speak the truth. It is well for you. What oath
will you swear never to return; and never to lead any living
creature hither by word or sign?'

'Master knows,' said Gollum with a sidelong glance at
Frodo. 'Yes, he knows. We will promise Master, if he saves
us. We'll promise to It, yes.' He crawled to Frodo's feet.
'Save us, nice Master!' he whined. 'Sméagol promises to
Precious, promises faithfully. Never come again, never speak,
no never! No, precious, no!'

'Are you satisfied?' said Faramir.

'Yes,' said Frodo. 'At least, you must either accept this
promise or carry out your law. You will get no more. But I
promised that if he came to me, he should not be harmed.
And I would not be proved faithless.'

Faramir sat for a moment in thought. 'Very good,' he said
at last. 'I surrender you to your master, to Frodo son of
Drogo. Let him declare what he will do with you!'

'But, Lord Faramir,' said Frodo bowing, 'you have not yet
declared your will concerning the said Frodo, and until that
is made known, he cannot shape his plans for himself or

his companions. Your judgement was postponed until the morning; but that is now at hand.'

'Then I will declare my doom,' said Faramir. 'As for you, Frodo, in so far as lies in me under higher authority, I declare you free in the realm of Gondor to the furthest of its ancient bounds; save only that neither you nor any that go with you have leave to come to this place unbidden. This doom shall stand for a year and a day, and then cease, unless you shall before that term come to Minas Tirith and present yourself to the Lord and Steward of the City. Then I will entreat him to confirm what I have done and to make it lifelong. In the meantime, whomsoever you take under your protection shall be under my protection and under the shield of Gondor. Are you answered?'

Frodo bowed low. 'I am answered,' he said, 'and I place myself at your service, if that is of any worth to one so high and honourable.'

'It is of great worth,' said Faramir. 'And now, do you take this creature, this Sméagol, under your protection?'

'I do take Sméagol under my protection,' said Frodo. Sam sighed audibly; and not at the courtesies, of which, as any hobbit would, he thoroughly approved. Indeed in the Shire such a matter would have required a great many more words and bows.

'Then I say to you,' said Faramir, turning to Gollum, 'you are under doom of death; but while you walk with Frodo you are safe for our part. Yet if ever you be found by any man of Gondor astray without him, the doom shall fall. And may death find you swiftly, within Gondor or without, if you do not well serve him. Now answer me: whither would you go? You were his guide, he says. Whither were you leading him?' Gollum made no reply.

'This I will not have secret,' said Faramir. 'Answer me, or I will reverse my judgement!' Still Gollum did not answer.

'I will answer for him,' said Frodo. 'He brought me to the Black Gate, as I asked; but it was impassable.'

'There is no open gate into the Nameless Land,' said Faramir.

'Seeing this, we turned aside and came by the Southward road,' Frodo continued; 'for he said that there is, or there may be, a path near to Minas Ithil.'

'Minas Morgul,' said Faramir.

'I do not know clearly,' said Frodo; 'but the path climbs, I think, up into the mountains on the northern side of that vale where the old city stands. It goes up to a high cleft and so down to – that which is beyond.'

'Do you know the name of that high pass?' said Faramir.

'No,' said Frodo.

'It is called Cirith Ungol.' Gollum hissed sharply and began muttering to himself. 'Is not that its name?' said Faramir turning to him.

'No!' said Gollum, and then he squealed, as if something had stabbed him. 'Yes, yes, we heard the name once. But what does the name matter to us? Master says he must get in. So we must try some way. There is no other way to try, no.'

'No other way?' said Faramir. 'How do you know that? And who has explored all the confines of that dark realm?' He looked long and thoughtfully at Gollum. Presently he spoke again. 'Take this creature away, Anborn. Treat him gently, but watch him. And do not you, Sméagol, try to dive into the falls. The rocks have such teeth there as would slay you before your time. Leave us now and take your fish!'

Anborn went out and Gollum went cringing before him. The curtain was drawn across the recess.

'Frodo, I think you do very unwisely in this,' said Faramir. 'I do not think you should go with this creature. It is wicked.'

'No, not altogether wicked,' said Frodo.

'Not wholly, perhaps,' said Faramir; 'but malice eats it like a canker, and the evil is growing. He will lead you to no good. If you will part with him, I will give him safe-conduct and guidance to any point on the borders of Gondor that he may name.'

'He would not take it,' said Frodo. 'He would follow after me as he long has done. And I have promised many times to take him under my protection and to go where he led. You would not ask me to break faith with him?'

'No,' said Faramir. 'But my heart would. For it seems less evil to counsel another man to break troth than to do so oneself, especially if one sees a friend bound unwitting to his own harm. But no – if he will go with you, you must now endure him. But I do not think you are holden to go to Cirith Ungol, of which he has told you less than he knows. That much I perceived clearly in his mind. Do not go to Cirith Ungol!'

'Where then shall I go?' said Frodo. 'Back to the Black Gate and deliver myself up to the guard? What do you know against this place that makes its name so dreadful?'

'Nothing certain,' said Faramir. 'We of Gondor do not ever pass east of the Road in these days, and none of us younger men has ever done so, nor has any of us set foot upon the Mountains of Shadow. Of them we know only old report and the rumour of bygone days. But there is some dark terror that dwells in the passes above Minas Morgul. If Cirith Ungol is named, old men and masters of lore will blanch and fall silent.

'The valley of Minas Morgul passed into evil very long ago, and it was a menace and a dread while the banished Enemy dwelt yet far away, and Ithilien was still for the most part in our keeping. As you know, that city was once a strong place, proud and fair, Minas Ithil, the twin sister of our own city. But it was taken by fell men whom the Enemy in his first strength had dominated, and who wandered homeless and masterless after his fall. It is said that their lords were men of Númenor who had fallen into dark wickedness; to them the Enemy had given rings of power, and he had devoured them: living ghosts they were become, terrible and evil. After his going they took Minas Ithil and dwelt there, and they filled it, and all the valley about, with decay: it seemed empty and was not so, for a shapeless fear lived within the ruined walls. Nine Lords there were, and after the return of their Master, which they aided and prepared in secret, they grew strong again. Then the Nine Riders issued forth from the gates of horror, and we could not withstand them. Do not approach their citadel. You will be espied. It is a place of sleepless malice, full of lidless eyes. Do not go that way!'

'But where else will you direct me?' said Frodo. 'You cannot yourself, you say, guide me to the mountains, nor over them. But over the mountains I am bound, by solemn undertaking to the Council, to find a way or perish in the seeking. And if I turn back, refusing the road in its bitter end, where then shall I go among Elves or Men? Would you have me come to Gondor with this Thing, the Thing that drove your brother mad with desire? What spell would it work in Minas Tirith? Shall there be two cities of Minas Morgul, grinning at each other across a dead land filled with rottenness?'

'I would not have it so,' said Faramir.

'Then what would you have me do?'

'I know not. Only I would not have you go to death or to torment. And I do not think that Mithrandir would have chosen this way.'

'Yet since he is gone, I must take such paths as I can find. And there is no time for long searching,' said Frodo.

'It is a hard doom and a hopeless errand,' said Faramir. 'But at the least, remember my warning: beware of this guide, Sméagol. He has done murder before now. I read it in him.' He sighed.

'Well, so we meet and part, Frodo son of Drogo. You have no need of soft words: I do not hope to see you again on any other day under this Sun. But you shall go now with my blessing upon you, and upon all your people. Rest a little while food is prepared for you.

'I would gladly learn how this creeping Sméagol became possessed of the Thing of which we speak, and how he lost it, but I will not trouble you now. If ever beyond hope you return to the lands of the living and we re-tell our tales, sitting

by a wall in the sun, laughing at old grief, you shall tell me
then. Until that time, or some other time beyond the vision
of the Seeing-stones of Númenor, farewell!'

He rose and bowed low to Frodo, and drawing the curtain
passed out into the cave.

CHAPTER VII

JOURNEY TO THE CROSS-ROADS

Frodo and Sam returned to their beds and lay there in silence
resting for a little, while men bestirred themselves and the
business of the day began. After a while water was brought
to them, and then they were led to a table where food was
set for three. Faramir broke his fast with them. He had not
slept since the battle on the day before, yet he did not look
weary.

When they had finished they stood up. 'May no hunger
trouble you on the road,' said Faramir. 'You have little pro-
vision, but some small store of food fit for travellers I have
ordered to be stowed in your packs. You will have no lack
of water as you walk in Ithilien, but do not drink of any
stream that flows from Imlad Morgul, the Valley of Living
Death. This also I must tell you. My scouts and watchers
have all returned, even some that have crept within sight of
the Morannon. They all find a strange thing. The land is
empty. Nothing is on the road, and no sound of foot, or
horn, or bowstring is anywhere to be heard. A waiting silence
broods above the Nameless Land. I do not know what this
portends. But the time draws swiftly to some great con-
clusion. Storm is coming. Hasten while you may! If you are
ready, let us go. The Sun will soon rise above the shadow.'

The hobbits' packs were brought to them (a little heavier
than they had been), and also two stout staves of polished
wood, shod with iron, and with carven heads through which
ran plaited leathern thongs.

'I have no fitting gifts to give you at our parting,' said
Faramir; 'but take these staves. They may be of service to
those who walk or climb in the wild. The men of the White
Mountains use them; though these have been cut down to

your height and newly shod. They are made of the fair tree *lebethron*, beloved of the woodwrights of Gondor, and a virtue has been set upon them of finding and returning. May that virtue not wholly fail under the Shadow into which you go!'

The hobbits bowed low. 'Most gracious host,' said Frodo, 'it was said to me by Elrond Halfelven that I should find friendship upon the way, secret and unlooked for. Certainly I looked for no such friendship as you have shown. To have found it turns evil to great good.'

Now they made ready to depart. Gollum was brought out of some corner or hiding-hole, and he seemed better pleased with himself than he had been, though he kept close to Frodo and avoided the glance of Faramir.

'Your guide must be blindfolded,' said Faramir, 'but you and your servant Samwise I release from this, if you wish.'

Gollum squealed, and squirmed, and clutched at Frodo, when they came to bind his eyes; and Frodo said: 'Blindfold us all three, and cover up my eyes first, and then perhaps he will see that no harm is meant.' This was done, and they were led from the cave of Henneth Annûn. After they had passed the passages and stairs they felt the cool morning air, fresh and sweet, about them. Still blind they went on for some little time, up and then gently down. At last the voice of Faramir ordered them to be uncovered.

They stood under the boughs of the woods again. No noise of the falls could be heard, for a long southward slope lay now between them and the ravine in which the stream flowed. To the west they could see light through the trees, as if the world came there to a sudden end, at a brink looking out only on to sky.

'Here is the last parting of our ways,' said Faramir. 'If you take my counsel, you will not turn eastward yet. Go straight on, for thus you will have the cover of the woodland for many miles. On your west is an edge where the land falls into the great vales, sometimes suddenly and sheer, sometimes in long hillsides. Keep near to this edge and the skirts of the forest. In the beginning of your journey you may walk under daylight, I think. The land dreams in a false peace, and for a while all evil is withdrawn. Fare you well, while you may!'

He embraced the hobbits then, after the manner of his people, stooping, and placing his hands upon their shoulders, and kissing their foreheads. 'Go with the good will of all good men!' he said.

They bowed to the ground. Then he turned and without looking back he left them and went to his two guards that stood at a little distance away. They marvelled to see with what speed these green-clad men now moved, vanishing almost in the twinkling of an eye. The forest where Faramir had stood seemed empty and drear, as if a dream had passed.

Frodo sighed and turned back southward. As if to mark his disregard of all such courtesy, Gollum was scrabbling in the mould at the foot of a tree. 'Hungry again already?' thought Sam. 'Well, now for it again!'

'Have they gone at last?' said Gollum. 'Nassty wicked Men! Sméagol's neck still hurts him, yes it does. Let's go!'

'Yes, let us go,' said Frodo. 'But if you can only speak ill of those who showed you mercy, keep silent!'

'Nice Master!' said Gollum. 'Sméagol was only joking. Always forgives, he does, yes, yes, even nice Master's little trickses. Oh yes, nice Master, nice Sméagol!'

Frodo and Sam did not answer. Hoisting their packs and taking their staves in hand, they passed on into the woods of Ithilien.

Twice that day they rested and took a little of the food provided by Faramir: dried fruits and salted meat, enough for many days; and bread enough to last while it was still fresh. Gollum ate nothing.

The sun rose and passed overhead unseen, and began to sink, and the light through the trees to the west grew golden; and always they walked in cool green shadow, and all about them was silence. The birds seemed all to have flown away or to have fallen dumb.

Darkness came early to the silent woods, and before the
fall of night they halted, weary, for they had walked seven
leagues or more from Henneth Annûn. Frodo lay and slept
away the night on the deep mould beneath an ancient tree.
Sam beside him was more uneasy: he woke many times, but
there was never a sign of Gollum, who had slipped off as
soon as the others had settled to rest. Whether he had slept
by himself in some hole nearby, or had wandered restlessly
prowling through the night, he did not say; but he returned
with the first glimmer of light, and roused his companions.

'Must get up, yes they must!' he said. 'Long ways to go
still, south and east. Hobbits must make haste!'

That day passed much as the day before had gone, except
that the silence seemed deeper; the air grew heavy, and it
began to be stifling under the trees. It felt as if thunder was
brewing. Gollum often paused, sniffing the air, and then he
would mutter to himself and urge them to greater speed.

As the third stage of their day's march drew on and afternoon waned, the forest opened out, and the trees became
larger and more scattered. Great ilexes of huge girth stood
dark and solemn in wide glades with here and there among
them hoary ash-trees, and giant oaks just putting out their
brown-green buds. About them lay long launds of green grass
dappled with celandine and anemones, white and blue, now
folded for sleep; and there were acres populous with the
leaves of woodland hyacinths: already their sleek bell-stems
were thrusting through the mould. No living creature, beast
or bird, was to be seen, but in these open places Gollum
grew afraid, and they walked now with caution, flitting from
one long shadow to another.

Light was fading fast when they came to the forest-end.
There they sat under an old gnarled oak that sent its roots
twisting like snakes down a steep crumbling bank. A deep
dim valley lay before them. On its further side the woods
gathered again, blue and grey under the sullen evening, and
marched on southwards. To the right the Mountains of

Gondor glowed, remote in the West, under a fire-flecked sky. To the left lay darkness: the towering walls of Mordor; and out of that darkness the long valley came, falling steeply in an ever-widening trough towards the Anduin. At its bottom ran a hurrying stream: Frodo could hear its stony voice coming up through the silence; and beside it on the hither side a road went winding down like a pale ribbon, down into chill grey mists that no gleam of sunset touched. There it seemed to Frodo that he descried far off, floating as it were on a shadowy sea, the high dim tops and broken pinnacles of old towers forlorn and dark.

He turned to Gollum. 'Do you know where we are?' he said.

'Yes, Master. Dangerous places. This is the road from the Tower of the Moon, Master, down to the ruined city by the shores of the River. The ruined city, yes, very nasty place, full of enemies. We shouldn't have taken Men's advice. Hobbits have come a long way out of the path. Must go east now, away up there.' He waved his skinny arm towards the darkling mountains. 'And we can't use this road. Oh no! Cruel peoples come this way, down from the Tower.'

Frodo looked down on to the road. At any rate nothing was moving on it now. It appeared lonely and forsaken, running down to empty ruins in the mist. But there was an evil feeling in the air, as if things might indeed be passing up and down that eyes could not see. Frodo shuddered as he looked again at the distant pinnacles now dwindling into night, and the sound of the water seemed cold and cruel: the voice of Morgulduin, the polluted stream that flowed from the Valley of the Wraiths.

'What shall we do?' he said. 'We have walked long and far. Shall we look for some place in the woods behind where we can lie hidden?'

'No good hiding in the dark,' said Gollum. 'It's in day that hobbits must hide now, yes in day.'

'Oh come!' said Sam. 'We must rest for a bit, even if we get up again in the middle of the night. There'll still be hours

of dark then, time enough for you to take us a long march,
if you know the way.'

Gollum reluctantly agreed to this, and he turned back
towards the trees, working eastward for a while along the
straggling edges of the wood. He would not rest on the
ground so near the evil road, and after some debate they all
climbed up into the crotch of a large holm-oak, whose thick
branches springing together from the trunk made a good
hiding-place and a fairly comfortable refuge. Night fell and
it grew altogether dark under the canopy of the tree. Frodo
and Sam drank a little water and ate some bread and dried
fruit, but Gollum at once curled up and went to sleep. The
hobbits did not shut their eyes.

It must have been a little after midnight when Gollum
woke up: suddenly they were aware of his pale eyes unlidded
gleaming at them. He listened and sniffed, which seemed, as
they had noticed before, his usual method of discovering the
time of night.

'Are we rested? Have we had beautiful sleep?' he said.
'Let's go!'

'We aren't, and we haven't,' growled Sam. 'But we'll go
if we must.'

Gollum dropped at once from the branches of the tree on
to all fours, and the hobbits followed more slowly.

As soon as they were down they went on again with Gollum
leading, eastwards, up the dark sloping land. They could see
little, for the night was now so deep that they were hardly
aware of the stems of trees before they stumbled against
them. The ground became more broken and walking was
more difficult, but Gollum seemed in no way troubled. He
led them through thickets and wastes of brambles; sometimes
round the lip of a deep cleft or dark pit, sometimes down
into black bush-shrouded hollows and out again; but if ever
they went a little downward, always the further slope was
longer and steeper. They were climbing steadily. At their first
halt they looked back, and they could dimly perceive the

roofs of the forest they had left behind, lying like a vast dense shadow, a darker night under the dark blank sky. There seemed to be a great blackness looming slowly out of the East, eating up the faint blurred stars. Later the sinking moon escaped from the pursuing cloud, but it was ringed all about with a sickly yellow glare.

At last Gollum turned to the hobbits. 'Day soon,' he said. 'Hobbits must hurry. Not safe to stay in the open in these places. Make haste!'

He quickened his pace, and they followed him wearily. Soon they began to climb up on to a great hog-back of land. For the most part it was covered with a thick growth of gorse and whortleberry, and low tough thorns, though here and there clearings opened, the scars of recent fires. The gorse-bushes became more frequent as they got nearer the top; very old and tall they were, gaunt and leggy below but thick above, and already putting out yellow flowers that glimmered in the gloom and gave a faint sweet scent. So tall were the spiny thickets that the hobbits could walk upright under them, passing through long dry aisles carpeted with a deep prickly mould.

On the further edge of this broad hill-back they stayed their march and crawled for hiding underneath a tangled knot of thorns. Their twisted boughs, stooping to the ground, were overridden by a clambering maze of old briars. Deep inside there was a hollow hall, raftered with dead branch and bramble, and roofed with the first leaves and shoots of spring. There they lay for a while, too tired yet to eat; and peering out through the holes in the covert they watched for the slow growth of day.

But no day came, only a dead brown twilight. In the East there was a dull red glare under the lowering cloud: it was not the red of dawn. Across the tumbled lands between, the mountains of the Ephel Dúath frowned at them, black and shapeless below where night lay thick and did not pass away, above with jagged tops and edges outlined hard and menacing against the fiery glow. Away to their right a great shoulder of the mountains stood out, dark and black amid the shadows, thrusting westward.

'Which way do we go from here?' asked Frodo. 'Is that the opening of – of the Morgul Valley, away over there beyond that black mass?'

'Need we think about it yet?' said Sam. 'Surely we're not going to move any more today, if day it is?'

'Perhaps not, perhaps not,' said Gollum. 'But we must go soon, to the Cross-roads. Yes, to the Cross-roads. That's the way over there, yes, Master.'

The red glare over Mordor died away. The twilight deepened as great vapours rose in the East and crawled above them. Frodo and Sam took a little food and then lay down, but Gollum was restless. He would not eat any of their food, but he drank a little water and then crawled about under the bushes, sniffing and muttering. Then suddenly he disappeared.

'Off hunting, I suppose,' said Sam and yawned. It was his turn to sleep first, and he was soon deep in a dream. He thought he was back in the Bag End garden looking for something; but he had a heavy pack on his back, which made him stoop. It all seemed very weedy and rank somehow, and thorns and bracken were invading the beds down near the bottom hedge.

'A job of work for me, I can see; but I'm so tired,' he kept on saying. Presently he remembered what he was looking for. 'My pipe!' he said, and with that he woke up.

'Silly!' he said to himself, as he opened his eyes and wondered why he was lying down under the hedge. 'It's in your pack all the time!' Then he realized, first that the pipe might be in his pack but he had no leaf, and next that he was hundreds of miles from Bag End. He sat up. It seemed to be almost dark. Why had his master let him sleep on out of turn, right on till evening?

'Haven't you had no sleep, Mr. Frodo?' he said. 'What's the time? Seems to be getting late!'

'No it isn't,' said Frodo. 'But the day is getting darker instead of lighter: darker and darker. As far as I can tell, it isn't midday yet, and you've only slept for about three hours.'

'I wonder what's up,' said Sam. 'Is there a storm coming? If so it's going to be the worst there ever was. We shall wish we were down a deep hole, not just stuck under a hedge.' He listened. 'What's that? Thunder, or drums, or what is it?'

'I don't know,' said Frodo. 'It's been going on for a good while now. Sometimes the ground seems to tremble, sometimes it seems to be the heavy air throbbing in your ears.'

Sam looked round. 'Where's Gollum?' he said. 'Hasn't he come back yet?'

'No,' said Frodo. 'There's not been a sign or sound of him.'

'Well, I can't abide him,' said Sam. 'In fact, I've never taken anything on a journey that I'd have been less sorry to lose on the way. But it would be just like him, after coming all these miles, to go and get lost now, just when we shall need him most – that is, if he's ever going to be any use, which I doubt.'

'You forget the Marshes,' said Frodo. 'I hope nothing has happened to him.'

'And I hope he's up to no tricks. And anyway I hope he doesn't fall into other hands, as you might say. Because if he does, we shall soon be in for trouble.'

At that moment a rolling and rumbling noise was heard again, louder now and deeper. The ground seemed to quiver under their feet. 'I think we are in for trouble anyhow,' said Frodo. 'I'm afraid our journey is drawing to an end.'

'Maybe,' said Sam; 'but *where there's life there's hope*, as my Gaffer used to say; *and need of vittles*, as he mostways used to add. You have a bite, Mr. Frodo, and then a bit of sleep.'

The afternoon, as Sam supposed it must be called, wore on. Looking out from the covert he could see only a dun, shadowless world, fading slowly into a featureless, colourless gloom. It felt stifling but not warm. Frodo slept unquietly, turning and tossing, and sometimes murmuring. Twice Sam thought he heard him speaking Gandalf's name. The time seemed to drag interminably. Suddenly Sam heard a hiss behind him, and there was Gollum on all fours, peering at them with gleaming eyes.

'Wake up, wake up! Wake up, sleepies!' he whispered. 'Wake up! No time to lose. We must go, yes, we must go at once. No time to lose!'

Sam stared at him suspiciously: he seemed frightened or excited. 'Go now? What's your little game? It isn't time yet. It can't be tea-time even, leastways not in decent places where there is tea-time.'

'Silly!' hissed Gollum. 'We're not in decent places. Time's running short, yes, running fast. No time to lose. We must go. Wake up, Master, wake up!' He clawed at Frodo; and Frodo, startled out of sleep, sat up suddenly and seized him by the arm. Gollum tore himself loose and backed away.

'They mustn't be silly,' he hissed. 'We must go. No time to lose!' And nothing more could they get out of him. Where he had been, and what he thought was brewing to make him in such a hurry, he would not say. Sam was filled with deep suspicion, and showed it; but Frodo gave no sign of what was passing in his mind. He sighed, hoisted his pack, and prepared to go out into the ever-gathering darkness.

Very stealthily Gollum led them down the hillside, keeping under cover wherever it was possible, and running, almost bent to the ground, across any open space; but the light was now so dim that even a keen-eyed beast of the wild could scarcely have seen the hobbits, hooded, in their grey cloaks, nor heard them, walking as warily as the little people can. Without the crack of a twig or the rustle of a leaf they passed and vanished.

For about an hour they went on, silently, in single file, oppressed by the gloom and by the absolute stillness of the land, broken only now and again by the faint rumbling as of thunder far away or drumbeats in some hollow of the hills.

Down from their hiding-place they went, and then turning
south they steered as straight a course as Gollum could find
across a long broken slope that leaned up towards the mountains. Presently, not far ahead, looming up like a black wall,
they saw a belt of trees. As they drew nearer they became
aware that these were of vast size, very ancient it seemed,
and still towering high, though their tops were gaunt and
broken, as if tempest and lightning-blast had swept across
them, but had failed to kill them or to shake their fathomless
roots.

'The Cross-roads, yes,' whispered Gollum, the first words
that had been spoken since they left their hiding-place. 'We
must go that way.' Turning eastward now, he led them up
the slope; and then suddenly there it was before them: the
Southward Road, winding its way about the outer feet of the
mountains, until presently it plunged into the great ring of
trees.

'This is the only way,' whispered Gollum. 'No paths
beyond the road. No paths. We must go to the Cross-roads.
But make haste! Be silent!'

As furtively as scouts within the campment of their
enemies, they crept down on to the road, and stole along
its westward edge under the stony bank, grey as the stones
themselves, and soft-footed as hunting cats. At length they
reached the trees, and found that they stood in a great roofless
ring, open in the middle to the sombre sky; and the spaces
between their immense boles were like the great dark arches
of some ruined hall. In the very centre four ways met. Behind
them lay the road to the Morannon; before them it ran out
again upon its long journey south; to their right the road
from old Osgiliath came climbing up, and crossing, passed
out eastward into darkness: the fourth way, the road they
were to take.

Standing there for a moment filled with dread Frodo
became aware that a light was shining; he saw it glowing on
Sam's face beside him. Turning towards it, he saw, beyond
an arch of boughs, the road to Osgiliath running almost as

straight as a stretched ribbon down, down, into the West. There, far away, beyond sad Gondor now overwhelmed in shade, the Sun was sinking, finding at last the hem of the great slow-rolling pall of cloud, and falling in an ominous fire towards the yet unsullied Sea. The brief glow fell upon a huge sitting figure, still and solemn as the great stone kings of Argonath. The years had gnawed it, and violent hands had maimed it. Its head was gone, and in its place was set in mockery a round rough-hewn stone, rudely painted by savage hands in the likeness of a grinning face with one large red eye in the midst of its forehead. Upon its knees and mighty chair, and all about the pedestal, were idle scrawls mixed with the foul symbols that the maggot-folk of Mordor used.

Suddenly, caught by the level beams, Frodo saw the old king's head: it was lying rolled away by the roadside. 'Look, Sam!' he cried, startled into speech. 'Look! The king has got a crown again!'

The eyes were hollow and the carven beard was broken, but about the high stern forehead there was a coronal of silver and gold. A trailing plant with flowers like small white stars had bound itself across the brows as if in reverence for the fallen king, and in the crevices of his stony hair yellow stonecrop gleamed.

'They cannot conquer for ever!' said Frodo. And then suddenly the brief glimpse was gone. The Sun dipped and vanished, and as if at the shuttering of a lamp, black night fell.

CHAPTER VIII

THE STAIRS OF CIRITH UNGOL

Gollum was tugging at Frodo's cloak and hissing with fear and impatience. 'We must go,' he said. 'We mustn't stand here. Make haste!'

Reluctantly Frodo turned his back on the West and followed as his guide led him, out into the darkness of the East. They left the ring of trees and crept along the road towards the mountains. This road, too, ran straight for a while, but soon it began to bend away southwards, until it came right under the great shoulder of rock that they had seen from the distance. Black and forbidding it loomed above them, darker than the dark sky behind. Crawling under its shadow the road went on, and rounding it sprang east again and began to climb steeply.

Frodo and Sam were plodding along with heavy hearts, no longer able to care greatly about their peril. Frodo's head was bowed; his burden was dragging him down again. As soon as the great Cross-roads had been passed, the weight of it, almost forgotten in Ithilien, had begun to grow once more. Now, feeling the way become steep before his feet, he looked wearily up; and then he saw it, even as Gollum had said that he would: the city of the Ringwraiths. He cowered against the stony bank.

A long-tilted valley, a deep gulf of shadow, ran back far into the mountains. Upon the further side, some way within the valley's arms, high on a rocky seat upon the black knees of the Ephel Dúath, stood the walls and tower of Minas Morgul. All was dark about it, earth and sky, but it was lit with light. Not the imprisoned moonlight welling through the marble walls of Minas Ithil long ago, Tower of the Moon, fair and radiant in the hollow of the hills. Paler indeed than the moon ailing in some slow eclipse was the light of it now, wavering and blowing like a noisome exhalation of decay, a corpse-light, a light that illuminated nothing. In the walls and tower windows showed, like countless black holes looking inward into emptiness; but the topmost course of the tower revolved slowly, first one way and then another, a huge ghostly head leering into the night. For a moment the three companions stood there, shrinking, staring up with unwilling eyes. Gollum was the first to recover. Again he pulled at their cloaks urgently, but he spoke no word. Almost he dragged them forward. Every step was reluctant, and time seemed to slow its pace, so that between the raising of a foot and the setting of it down minutes of loathing passed.

So they came slowly to the white bridge. Here the road, gleaming faintly, passed over the stream in the midst of the valley, and went on, winding deviously up towards the city's gate: a black mouth opening in the outer circle of the north-ward walls. Wide flats lay on either bank, shadowy meads filled with pale white flowers. Luminous these were too, beautiful and yet horrible of shape, like the demented forms in an uneasy dream; and they gave forth a faint sickening charnel-smell; an odour of rottenness filled the air. From mead to mead the bridge sprang. Figures stood there at its head, carven with cunning in forms human and bestial, but all corrupt and loathsome. The water flowing beneath was silent, and it steamed, but the vapour that rose from it, curling and twisting about the bridge, was deadly cold. Frodo felt his senses reeling and his mind darkening. Then suddenly, as if some force were at work other than his own will, he began to hurry, tottering forward, his groping hands held out, his head lolling from side to side. Both Sam and Gollum ran after him. Sam caught his master in his arms, as he stumbled and almost fell, right on the threshold of the bridge.

'Not that way! No, not that way!' whispered Gollum, but the breath between his teeth seemed to tear the heavy stillness like a whistle, and he cowered to the ground in terror.

'Hold up, Mr. Frodo!' muttered Sam in Frodo's ear. 'Come

back! Not that way. Gollum says not, and for once I agree
with him.'

Frodo passed his hand over his brow and wrenched his
eyes away from the city on the hill. The luminous tower
fascinated him, and he fought the desire that was on him to
run up the gleaming road towards its gate. At last with an
effort he turned back, and as he did so, he felt the Ring
resisting him, dragging at the chain about his neck; and his
eyes too, as he looked away, seemed for the moment to have
been blinded. The darkness before him was impenetrable.

Gollum, crawling on the ground like a frightened animal,
was already vanishing into the gloom. Sam, supporting and
guiding his stumbling master, followed after him as quickly
as he could. Not far from the near bank of the stream there
was a gap in the stone-wall beside the road. Through this
they passed, and Sam saw that they were on a narrow path
that gleamed faintly at first, as the main road did, until climbing above the meads of deadly flowers it faded and went
dark, winding its crooked way up into the northern sides of
the valley.

Along this path the hobbits trudged, side by side, unable
to see Gollum in front of them, except when he turned back
to beckon them on. Then his eyes shone with a green-white
light, reflecting the noisome Morgul-sheen perhaps, or
kindled by some answering mood within. Of that deadly
gleam and of the dark eyeholes Frodo and Sam were always
conscious, ever glancing fearfully over their shoulders, and
ever dragging their eyes back to find the darkening path.
Slowly they laboured on. As they rose above the stench and
vapours of the poisonous stream their breath became easier
and their heads clearer; but now their limbs were deadly tired,
as if they had walked all night under a burden, or had been
swimming long against a heavy tide of water. At last they
could go no further without a halt.

Frodo stopped and sat down on a stone. They had now
climbed up to the top of a great hump of bare rock. Ahead
of them there was a bay in the valley-side, and round the

head of this the path went on, no more than a wide ledge
with a chasm on the right; across the sheer southward face
of the mountain it crawled upwards, until it disappeared into
the blackness above.

'I must rest a while, Sam,' whispered Frodo. 'It's heavy
on me, Sam lad, very heavy. I wonder how far I can carry
it? Anyway I must rest before we venture on to that.' He
pointed to the narrow way ahead.

'Sssh! ssh!' hissed Gollum hurrying back to them. 'Sssh!'
His fingers were on his lips and he shook his head urgently.
Tugging at Frodo's sleeve, he pointed towards the path; but
Frodo would not move.

'Not yet,' he said, 'not yet.' Weariness and more than
weariness oppressed him; it seemed as if a heavy spell was
laid on his mind and body. 'I must rest,' he muttered.

At this Gollum's fear and agitation became so great that
he spoke again, hissing behind his hand, as if to keep the
sound from unseen listeners in the air. 'Not here, no. Not
rest here. Fools! Eyes can see us. When they come to the
bridge they will see us. Come away! Climb, climb! Come!'

'Come, Mr. Frodo,' said Sam. 'He's right again. We can't
stay here.'

'All right,' said Frodo in a remote voice, as of one speaking
half asleep. 'I will try.' Wearily he got to his feet.

But it was too late. At that moment the rock quivered and
trembled beneath them. The great rumbling noise, louder
than ever before, rolled in the ground and echoed in the
mountains. Then with searing suddenness there came a great
red flash. Far beyond the eastern mountains it leapt into the
sky and splashed the lowering clouds with crimson. In that
valley of shadow and cold deathly light it seemed unbearably
violent and fierce. Peaks of stone and ridges like notched
knives sprang out in staring black against the uprushing flame
in Gorgoroth. Then came a great crack of thunder.

And Minas Morgul answered. There was a flare of livid
lightnings: forks of blue flame springing up from the tower

and from the encircling hills into the sullen clouds. The earth groaned; and out of the city there came a cry. Mingled with harsh high voices as of birds of prey, and the shrill neighing of horses wild with rage and fear, there came a rending screech, shivering, rising swiftly to a piercing pitch beyond the range of hearing. The hobbits wheeled round towards it, and cast themselves down, holding their hands upon their ears.

As the terrible cry ended, falling back through a long sickening wail to silence, Frodo slowly raised his head. Across the narrow valley, now almost on a level with his eyes, the walls of the evil city stood, and its cavernous gate, shaped like an open mouth with gleaming teeth, was gaping wide. And out of the gate an army came.

All that host was clad in sable, dark as the night. Against the wan walls and the luminous pavement of the road Frodo could see them, small black figures in rank upon rank, marching swiftly and silently, passing outwards in an endless stream. Before them went a great cavalry of horsemen moving like ordered shadows, and at their head was one greater than all the rest: a Rider, all black, save that on his hooded head he had a helm like a crown that flickered with a perilous light. Now he was drawing near the bridge below, and Frodo's staring eyes followed him, unable to wink or to withdraw. Surely there was the Lord of the Nine Riders returned to earth to lead his ghastly host to battle? Here, yes here indeed was the haggard king whose cold hand had smitten down the Ring-bearer with his deadly knife. The old wound throbbed with pain and a great chill spread towards Frodo's heart.

Even as these thoughts pierced him with dread and held him bound as with a spell, the Rider halted suddenly, right before the entrance of the bridge, and behind him all the host stood still. There was a pause, a dead silence. Maybe it was the Ring that called to the Wraith-lord, and for a moment he was troubled, sensing some other power within his valley. This way and that turned the dark head helmed and crowned with fear, sweeping the shadows with its unseen eyes. Frodo waited, like a bird at the approach of a snake, unable to move. And as he waited, he felt, more urgent than ever before, the command that he should put on the Ring. But great as the pressure was, he felt no inclination now to yield to it. He knew that the Ring would only betray him, and that he had not, even if he put it on, the power to face the Morgul-king – not yet. There was no longer any answer to that command in his own will, dismayed by terror though it was, and he felt only the beating upon him of a great power from outside. It took his hand, and as Frodo watched with his mind, not willing it but in suspense (as if he looked on some old story far away), it moved the hand inch by inch towards the chain upon his neck. Then his own will stirred; slowly it forced the hand back and set it to find another thing, a thing lying hidden near his breast. Cold and hard it seemed as his grip closed on it: the phial of Galadriel, so long treasured, and almost forgotten till that hour. As he touched it, for a while all thought of the Ring was banished from his mind. He sighed and bent his head.

At that moment the Wraith-king turned and spurred his horse and rode across the bridge, and all his dark host followed him. Maybe the elven-hoods defied his unseen eyes, and the mind of his small enemy, being strengthened, had turned aside his thought. But he was in haste. Already the hour had struck, and at his great Master's bidding he must march with war into the West.

Soon he had passed, like a shadow into shadow, down the winding road, and behind him still the black ranks crossed the bridge. So great an army had never issued from that vale since the days of Isildur's might; no host so fell and strong in arms had yet assailed the fords of Anduin; and yet it was but one and not the greatest of the hosts that Mordor now sent forth.

Frodo stirred. And suddenly his heart went out to Faramir. 'The storm has burst at last,' he thought. 'This great array of spears and swords is going to Osgiliath. Will Faramir get

across in time? He guessed it, but did he know the hour?
And who can now hold the fords when the King of the Nine
Riders comes? And other armies will come. I am too late.
All is lost. I tarried on the way. All is lost. Even if my errand
is performed, no one will ever know. There will be no one I
can tell. It will be in vain.' Overcome with weakness he wept.
And still the host of Morgul crossed the bridge.

Then at a great distance, as if it came out of memories of
the Shire, some sunlit early morning, when the day called
and doors were opening, he heard Sam's voice speaking.
'Wake up, Mr. Frodo! Wake up!' Had the voice added: 'Your
breakfast is ready,' he would hardly have been surprised.
Certainly Sam was urgent. 'Wake up, Mr. Frodo! They're
gone,' he said.

There was a dull clang. The gates of Minas Morgul had
closed. The last rank of spears had vanished down the road.
The tower still grinned across the valley, but the light was
fading in it. The whole city was falling back into a dark
brooding shade, and silence. Yet still it was filled with watchfulness.

'Wake up, Mr. Frodo! They're gone, and we'd better go
too. There's something still alive in that place, something
with eyes, or a seeing mind, if you take me; and the longer
we stay in one spot, the sooner it will get on to us. Come
on, Mr. Frodo!'

Frodo raised his head, and then stood up. Despair had not
left him, but the weakness had passed. He even smiled grimly,
feeling now as clearly as a moment before he had felt the
opposite, that what he had to do, he had to do, if he could,
and that whether Faramir or Aragorn or Elrond or Galadriel
or Gandalf or anyone else ever knew about it was beside the
purpose. He took his staff in one hand and the phial in his
other. When he saw that the clear light was already welling
through his fingers, he thrust it into his bosom and held it
against his heart. Then turning from the city of Morgul, now
no more than a grey glimmer across a dark gulf, he prepared
to take the upward road.

Gollum, it seemed, had crawled off along the ledge into the darkness beyond, when the gates of Minas Morgul opened, leaving the hobbits where they lay. He now came creeping back, his teeth chattering and his fingers snapping. 'Foolish! Silly!' he hissed. 'Make haste! They mustn't think danger has passed. It hasn't. Make haste!'

They did not answer, but they followed him on to the climbing ledge. It was little to the liking of either of them, not even after facing so many other perils; but it did not last long. Soon the path reached a rounded angle where the mountain-side swelled out again, and there it suddenly entered a narrow opening in the rock. They had come to the first stair that Gollum had spoken of. The darkness was almost complete, and they could see nothing much beyond their hands' stretch; but Gollum's eyes shone pale, several feet above, as he turned back towards them.

'Careful!' he whispered. 'Steps. Lots of steps. Must be careful!'

Care was certainly needed. Frodo and Sam at first felt easier, having now a wall on either side, but the stairway was almost as steep as a ladder, and as they climbed up and up, they became more and more aware of the long black fall behind them. And the steps were narrow, spaced unevenly, and often treacherous: they were worn and smooth at the edges, and some were broken, and some cracked as foot was set upon them. The hobbits struggled on, until at last they were clinging with desperate fingers to the steps ahead, and forcing their aching knees to bend and straighten; and ever as the stair cut its way deeper into the sheer mountain the rocky walls rose higher and higher above their heads.

At length, just as they felt that they could endure no more, they saw Gollum's eyes peering down at them again. 'We're up,' he whispered. 'First stair's past. Clever hobbits to climb so high, very clever hobbits. Just a few more little steps and that's all, yes.'

*   *   *

Dizzy and very tired Sam, and Frodo following him, crawled up the last step, and sat down rubbing their legs and knees. They were in a deep dark passage that seemed still to go up before them, though at a gentler slope and without steps. Gollum did not let them rest long.

'There's another stair still,' he said. 'Much longer stair. Rest when we get to the top of next stair. Not yet.'

Sam groaned. 'Longer, did you say?' he asked.

'Yes, yess, longer,' said Gollum. 'But not so difficult. Hobbits have climbed the Straight Stair. Next comes the Winding Stair.'

'And what after that?' said Sam.

'We shall see,' said Gollum softly. 'O yes, we shall see!'

'I thought you said there was a tunnel,' said Sam. 'Isn't there a tunnel or something to go through?'

'O yes, there's a tunnel,' said Gollum. 'But hobbits can rest before they try that. If they get through that, they'll be nearly at the top. Very nearly, if they get through. O yes!'

Frodo shivered. The climb had made him sweat, but now he felt cold and clammy, and there was a chill draught in the dark passage, blowing down from the invisible heights above. He got up and shook himself. 'Well, let's go on!' he said. 'This is no place to sit in.'

The passage seemed to go on for miles, and always the chill air flowed over them, rising as they went on to a bitter wind. The mountains seemed to be trying with their deadly breath to daunt them, to turn them back from the secrets of the high places, or to blow them away into the darkness behind. They only knew that they had come to the end, when suddenly they felt no wall at their right hand. They could see very little. Great black shapeless masses and deep grey shadows loomed above them and about them, but now and again a dull red light flickered up under the lowering clouds, and for a moment they were aware of tall peaks, in front and on either side, like pillars holding up a vast sagging roof. They seemed to have climbed up many hundreds of feet, on to a wide shelf. A cliff was on their left and a chasm on their right.

Gollum led the way close under the cliff. For the present they were no longer climbing, but the ground was now more broken and dangerous in the dark, and there were blocks and lumps of fallen stone in the way. Their going was slow and cautious. How many hours had passed since they had entered the Morgul Vale neither Sam nor Frodo could any longer guess. The night seemed endless.

At length they were once more aware of a wall looming up, and once more a stairway opened before them. Again they halted, and again they began to climb. It was a long and weary ascent; but this stairway did not delve into the mountain-side. Here the huge cliff-face sloped backwards, and the path like a snake wound to and fro across it. At one point it crawled sideways right to the edge of the dark chasm, and Frodo glancing down saw below him as a vast deep pit the great ravine at the head of the Morgul Valley. Down in its depths glimmered like a glow-worm thread the wraith-road from the dead city to the Nameless Pass. He turned hastily away.

Still on and up the stairway bent and crawled, until at last with a final flight, short and straight, it climbed out again on to another level. The path had veered away from the main pass in the great ravine, and it now followed its own perilous course at the bottom of a lesser cleft among the higher regions of the Ephel Dúath. Dimly the hobbits could discern tall piers and jagged pinnacles of stone on either side, between which were great crevices and fissures blacker than the night, where forgotten winters had gnawed and carved the sunless stone. And now the red light in the sky seemed stronger; though they could not tell whether a dreadful morning were indeed coming to this place of shadow, or whether they saw only the flame of some great violence of Sauron in the torment of Gorgoroth beyond. Still far ahead, and still high above, Frodo, looking up, saw, as he guessed, the very crown of this bitter road. Against the sullen redness of the eastern sky a cleft was outlined in the topmost ridge, narrow, deep-cloven between two black shoulders; and on either shoulder was a horn of stone.

He paused and looked more attentively. The horn upon the left was tall and slender; and in it burned a red light, or else the red light in the land beyond was shining through a hole. He saw now: it was a black tower poised above the outer pass. He touched Sam's arm and pointed.

'I don't like the look of that!' said Sam. 'So this secret way of yours is guarded after all,' he growled, turning to Gollum. 'As you knew all along, I suppose?'

'All ways are watched, yes,' said Gollum. 'Of course they are. But hobbits must try some way. This may be least watched. Perhaps they've all gone away to big battle, perhaps!'

'Perhaps,' grunted Sam. 'Well, it still seems a long way off, and a long way up before we get there. And there's still the tunnel. I think you ought to rest now, Mr. Frodo. I don't know what time of day or night it is, but we've kept going for hours and hours.'

'Yes, we must rest,' said Frodo. 'Let us find some corner out of the wind, and gather our strength – for the last lap.' For so he felt it to be. The terrors of the land beyond, and the deed to be done there, seemed remote, too far off yet to trouble him. All his mind was bent on getting through or over this impenetrable wall and guard. If once he could do that impossible thing, then somehow the errand would be accomplished, or so it seemed to him in that dark hour of weariness, still labouring in the stony shadows under Cirith Ungol.

In a dark crevice between two great piers of rock they sat down: Frodo and Sam a little way within, and Gollum crouched upon the ground near the opening. There the hob-bits took what they expected would be their last meal before they went down into the Nameless Land, maybe the last meal they would ever eat together. Some of the food of Gondor they ate, and wafers of the waybread of the Elves, and they drank a little. But of their water they were sparing and took only enough to moisten their dry mouths.

'I wonder when we'll find water again?' said Sam. 'But I suppose even over there they drink? Orcs drink, don't they?'

'Yes, they drink,' said Frodo. 'But do not let us speak of that. Such drink is not for us.'

'Then all the more need to fill our bottles,' said Sam. 'But there isn't any water up here: not a sound or a trickle have I heard. And anyway Faramir said we were not to drink any water in Morgul.'

'No water flowing out of Imlad Morgul, were his words,' said Frodo. 'We are not in that valley now, and if we came on a spring it would be flowing into it and not out of it.'

'I wouldn't trust it,' said Sam, 'not till I was dying of thirst. There's a wicked feeling about this place.' He sniffed. 'And a smell, I fancy. Do you notice it? A queer kind of a smell, stuffy. I don't like it.'

'I don't like anything here at all,' said Frodo, 'step or stone, breath or bone. Earth, air and water all seem accursed. But so our path is laid.'

'Yes, that's so,' said Sam. 'And we shouldn't be here at all, if we'd known more about it before we started. But I suppose it's often that way. The brave things in the old tales and songs, Mr. Frodo: adventures, as I used to call them. I used to think that they were things the wonderful folk of the stories went out and looked for, because they wanted them, because they were exciting and life was a bit dull, a kind of a sport, as you might say. But that's not the way of it with the tales that really mattered, or the ones that stay in the mind. Folk seem to have been just landed in them, usually – their paths were laid that way, as you put it. But I expect they had lots of chances, like us, of turning back, only they didn't. And if they had, we shouldn't know, because they'd have been forgotten. We hear about those as just went on – and not all to a good end, mind you; at least not to what folk inside a story and not outside it call a good end. You know, coming home, and finding things all right, though not quite the same – like old Mr. Bilbo. But those aren't always the best tales to hear, though they may be the best tales to get landed in! I wonder what sort of a tale we've fallen into?'

'I wonder,' said Frodo. 'But I don't know. And that's the way of a real tale. Take any one that you're fond of. You may know, or guess, what kind of a tale it is, happy-ending or sad-ending, but the people in it don't know. And you don't want them to.'

'No, sir, of course not. Beren now, he never thought he was going to get that Silmaril from the Iron Crown in Thangorodrim, and yet he did, and that was a worse place and a blacker danger than ours. But that's a long tale, of course, and goes on past the happiness and into grief and beyond it – and the Silmaril went on and came to Eärendil. And why, sir, I never thought of that before! We've got – you've got some of the light of it in that star-glass that the Lady gave you! Why, to think of it, we're in the same tale still! It's going on. Don't the great tales never end?'

'No, they never end as tales,' said Frodo. 'But the people in them come, and go when their part's ended. Our part will end later – or sooner.'

'And then we can have some rest and some sleep,' said Sam. He laughed grimly. 'And I mean just that, Mr. Frodo. I mean plain ordinary rest, and sleep, and waking up to a morning's work in the garden. I'm afraid that's all I'm hoping for all the time. All the big important plans are not for my sort. Still, I wonder if we shall ever be put into songs or tales. We're in one, of course; but I mean: put into words, you know, told by the fireside, or read out of a great big book with red and black letters, years and years afterwards. And people will say: "Let's hear about Frodo and the Ring!" And they'll say: "Yes, that's one of my favourite stories. Frodo was very brave, wasn't he, dad?" "Yes, my boy, the famousest of the hobbits, and that's saying a lot." '

'It's saying a lot too much,' said Frodo, and he laughed, a long clear laugh from his heart. Such a sound had not been heard in those places since Sauron came to Middle-earth. To Sam suddenly it seemed as if all the stones were listening and the tall rocks leaning over them. But Frodo did not heed them; he laughed again. 'Why, Sam,' he said, 'to hear you somehow makes me as merry as if the story was already written. But you've left out one of the chief characters: Samwise the stouthearted. "I want to hear more about Sam, dad. Why didn't they put in more of his talk, dad? That's what I like, it makes me laugh. And Frodo wouldn't have got far without Sam, would he, dad?"'

'Now, Mr. Frodo,' said Sam, 'you shouldn't make fun. I was serious.'

'So was I,' said Frodo, 'and so I am. We're going on a bit too fast. You and I, Sam, are still stuck in the worst places of the story, and it is all too likely that some will say at this point: "Shut the book now, dad; we don't want to read any more."'

'Maybe,' said Sam, 'but I wouldn't be one to say that. Things done and over and made into part of the great tales are different. Why, even Gollum might be good in a tale, better than he is to have by you, anyway. And he used to like tales himself once, by his own account. I wonder if he thinks he's the hero or the villain?

'Gollum!' he called. 'Would you like to be the hero – now where's he got to again?'

There was no sign of him at the mouth of their shelter nor in the shadows near. He had refused their food, though he had, as usual, accepted a mouthful of water; and then he had seemed to curl up for a sleep. They had supposed that one at any rate of his objects in his long absence the day before had been to hunt for food to his own liking; and now he had evidently slipped off again while they talked. But what for this time?

'I don't like his sneaking off without saying,' said Sam. 'And least of all now. He can't be looking for food up here, not unless there's some kind of rock he fancies. Why, there isn't even a bit of moss!'

'It's no good worrying about him now,' said Frodo. 'We couldn't have got so far, not even within sight of the pass, without him, and so we'll have to put up with his ways. If he's false, he's false.'

'All the same, I'd rather have him under my eye,' said Sam. 'All the more so, if he's false. Do you remember he never would say if this pass was guarded or no? And now we see a tower there – and it may be deserted, and it may not. Do you think he's gone to fetch them, Orcs or whatever they are?'

'No, I don't think so,' answered Frodo. 'Even if he's up to some wickedness, and I suppose that's not unlikely. I don't think it's that: not to fetch Orcs, or any servants of the Enemy. Why wait till now, and go through all the labour of the climb, and come so near the land he fears? He could probably have betrayed us to Orcs many times since we met him. No, if it's anything, it will be some little private trick of his own that he thinks is quite secret.'

'Well, I suppose you're right, Mr. Frodo,' said Sam. 'Not that it comforts me mightily. I don't make no mistake: I don't doubt he'd hand *me* over to Orcs as gladly as kiss his hand. But I was forgetting – his Precious. No, I suppose the whole time it's been *The Precious for poor Sméagol*. That's the one idea in all his little schemes, if he has any. But how bringing us up here will help him in that is more than I can guess.'

'Very likely he can't guess himself,' said Frodo. 'And I don't think he's got just one plain scheme in his muddled head. I think he really is in part trying to save the Precious from the Enemy, as long as he can. For that would be the last disaster for himself too, if the Enemy got it. And in the other part, perhaps, he's just biding his time and waiting on chance.'

'Yes, Slinker and Stinker, as I've said before,' said Sam. 'But the nearer they get to the Enemy's land the more like Stinker Slinker will get. Mark my words: if ever we get to the pass, he won't let us really take the precious thing over the border without making some kind of trouble.'

'We haven't got there yet,' said Frodo.

'No, but we'd better keep our eyes skinned till we do. If we're caught napping, Stinker will come out on top pretty quick. Not but what it would be safe for you to have a wink now, master. Safe, if you lay close to me. I'd be dearly glad to see you have a sleep. I'd keep watch over you; and anyway, if you lay near, with my arm round you, no one could come pawing you without your Sam knowing it.'

'Sleep!' said Frodo and sighed, as if out of a desert he had seen a mirage of cool green. 'Yes, even here I could sleep.'

'Sleep then, master! Lay your head in my lap.'

And so Gollum found them hours later, when he returned, crawling and creeping down the path out of the gloom ahead. Sam sat propped against the stone, his head dropping sideways and his breathing heavy. In his lap lay Frodo's head, drowned deep in sleep; upon his white forehead lay one of Sam's brown hands, and the other lay softly upon his master's breast. Peace was in both their faces.

Gollum looked at them. A strange expression passed over his lean hungry face. The gleam faded from his eyes, and they went dim and grey, old and tired. A spasm of pain seemed to twist him, and he turned away, peering back up towards the pass, shaking his head, as if engaged in some interior debate. Then he came back, and slowly putting out a trembling hand, very cautiously he touched Frodo's knee – but almost the touch was a caress. For a fleeting moment, could one of the sleepers have seen him, they would have thought that they beheld an old weary hobbit, shrunken by the years that had carried him far beyond his time, beyond friends and kin, and the fields and streams of youth, an old starved pitiable thing.

But at that touch Frodo stirred and cried out softly in his sleep, and immediately Sam was wide awake. The first thing he saw was Gollum – 'pawing at master,' as he thought.

'Hey you!' he said roughly. 'What are you up to?'

'Nothing, nothing,' said Gollum softly. 'Nice Master!'

'I daresay,' said Sam. 'But where have you been to – sneaking off and sneaking back, you old villain?'

Gollum withdrew himself, and a green glint flickered under his heavy lids. Almost spider-like he looked now, crouched back on his bent limbs, with his protruding eyes. The fleeting moment had passed, beyond recall. 'Sneaking, sneaking!' he hissed. 'Hobbits always so polite, yes. O nice hobbits! Sméagol brings them up secret ways that nobody else could find. Tired he is, thirsty he is, yes thirsty; and he guides them and he searches for paths, and they say *sneak, sneak*. Very nice friends, O yes my precious, very nice.'

Sam felt a bit remorseful, though not more trustful. 'Sorry,' he said. 'I'm sorry, but you startled me out of my sleep. And I shouldn't have been sleeping, and that made me a bit sharp. But Mr. Frodo, he's that tired, I asked him to have a wink; and well, that's how it is. Sorry. But where *have* you been to?'

'Sneaking,' said Gollum, and the green glint did not leave his eyes.

'O very well,' said Sam, 'have it your own way! I don't suppose it's so far from the truth. And now we'd better all be sneaking along together. What's the time? Is it today or tomorrow?'

'It's tomorrow,' said Gollum, 'or this was tomorrow when hobbits went to sleep. Very foolish, very dangerous – if poor Sméagol wasn't sneaking about to watch.'

'I think we shall get tired of that word soon,' said Sam. 'But never mind. I'll wake master up.' Gently he smoothed the hair back from Frodo's brow, and bending down spoke softly to him.

'Wake up, Mr. Frodo! Wake up!'

Frodo stirred and opened his eyes, and smiled, seeing Sam's face bending over him. 'Calling me early aren't you, Sam?' he said. 'It's dark still!'

'Yes it's always dark here,' said Sam. 'But Gollum's come

back, Mr. Frodo, and he says it's tomorrow. So we must be walking on. The last lap.'

Frodo drew a deep breath and sat up. 'The last lap!' he said. 'Hullo, Sméagol! Found any food? Have you had any rest?'

'No food, no rest, nothing for Sméagol,' said Gollum. 'He's a sneak.'

Sam clicked his tongue, but restrained himself.

'Don't take names to yourself, Sméagol,' said Frodo. 'It's unwise, whether they are true or false.'

'Sméagol has to take what's given him,' answered Gollum. 'He was given that name by kind Master Samwise, the hobbit that knows so much.'

Frodo looked at Sam. 'Yes sir,' he said. 'I did use the word, waking up out of my sleep sudden and all and finding him at hand. I said I was sorry, but I soon shan't be.'

'Come, let it pass then,' said Frodo. 'But now we seem to have come to the point, you and I, Sméagol. Tell me. Can we find the rest of the way by ourselves? We're in sight of the pass, of a way in, and if we can find it now, then I suppose our agreement can be said to be over. You have done what you promised, and you're free: free to go back to food and rest, wherever you wish to go, except to servants of the Enemy. And one day I may reward you, I or those that remember me.'

'No, no, not yet,' Gollum whined. 'O no! They can't find the way themselves, can they? O no indeed. There's the tunnel coming. Sméagol must go on. No rest. No food. Not yet.'

CHAPTER IX

SHELOB'S LAIR

It may indeed have been daytime now, as Gollum said, but the hobbits could see little difference, unless, perhaps, the heavy sky above was less utterly black, more like a great roof of smoke; while instead of the darkness of deep night, which lingered still in cracks and holes, a grey blurring shadow shrouded the stony world about them. They passed on, Gollum in front and the hobbits now side by side, up the long ravine between the piers and columns of torn and weathered rock, standing like huge unshapen statues on either hand. There was no sound. Some way ahead, a mile or so, perhaps, was a great grey wall, a last huge upthrusting mass of mountain-stone. Darker it loomed, and steadily it rose as they approached, until it towered up high above them, shutting out the view of all that lay beyond. Deep shadow lay before its feet. Sam sniffed the air.

'Ugh! That smell!' he said. 'It's getting stronger and stronger.'

Presently they were under the shadow, and there in the midst of it they saw the opening of a cave. 'This is the way in,' said Gollum softly. 'This is the entrance to the tunnel.' He did not speak its name: Torech Ungol, Shelob's Lair. Out of it came a stench, not the sickly odour of decay in the meads of Morgul, but a foul reek, as if filth unnameable were piled and hoarded in the dark within.

'Is this the only way, Sméagol?' said Frodo.

'Yes, yes,' he answered. 'Yes, we must go this way now.'

'D'you mean to say you've been through this hole?' said Sam. 'Phew! But perhaps you don't mind bad smells.'

Gollum's eyes glinted. 'He doesn't know what we minds, does he, precious? No, he doesn't. But Sméagol can bear things. Yes. He's been through. O yes, right through. It's the only way.'

'And what makes the smell, I wonder,' said Sam. 'It's like – well, I wouldn't like to say. Some beastly hole of the Orcs, I'll warrant, with a hundred years of their filth in it.'

'Well,' said Frodo, 'Orcs or no, if it's the only way, we must take it.'

Drawing a deep breath they passed inside. In a few steps they were in utter and impenetrable dark. Not since the lightless passages of Moria had Frodo or Sam known such darkness, and if possible here it was deeper and denser. There, there were airs moving, and echoes, and a sense of space. Here the air was still, stagnant, heavy, and sound fell dead. They walked as it were in a black vapour wrought of veritable darkness itself that, as it was breathed, brought blindness not only to the eyes but to the mind, so that even the memory of colours and of forms and of any light faded out of thought. Night always had been, and always would be, and night was all.

But for a while they could still feel, and indeed the senses of their feet and fingers at first seemed sharpened almost painfully. The walls felt, to their surprise, smooth, and the floor, save for a step now and again, was straight and even, going ever up at the same stiff slope. The tunnel was high and wide, so wide that, though the hobbits walked abreast, only touching the side-walls with their outstretched hands, they were separated, cut off alone in the darkness.

Gollum had gone in first and seemed to be only a few steps ahead. While they were still able to give heed to such things, they could hear his breath hissing and gasping just in front of them. But after a time their senses became duller, both touch and hearing seemed to grow numb, and they kept on, groping, walking, on and on, mainly by the force of the will with which they had entered, will to go through and desire to come at last to the high gate beyond.

Before they had gone very far, perhaps, but time and

distance soon passed out of his reckoning, Sam on the right, feeling the wall, was aware that there was an opening at the side: for a moment he caught a faint breath of some air less heavy, and then they passed it by.

'There's more than one passage here,' he whispered with an effort: it seemed hard to make his breath give any sound. 'It's as orc-like a place as ever there could be!'

After that, first he on the right, and then Frodo on the left, passed three or four such openings, some wider, some smaller; but there was as yet no doubt of the main way, for it was straight, and did not turn, and still went steadily up. But how long was it, how much more of this would they have to endure, or could they endure? The breathlessness of the air was growing as they climbed; and now they seemed often in the blind dark to sense some resistance thicker than the foul air. As they thrust forward they felt things brush against their heads, or against their hands, long tentacles, or hanging growths perhaps: they could not tell what they were. And still the stench grew. It grew, until almost it seemed to them that smell was the only clear sense left to them, and that was for their torment. One hour, two hours, three hours: how many had they passed in this lightless hole? Hours – days, weeks rather. Sam left the tunnel-side and shrank towards Frodo, and their hands met and clasped, and so together they still went on.

At length Frodo, groping along the left-hand wall, came suddenly to a void. Almost he fell sideways into the emptiness. Here was some opening in the rock far wider than any they had yet passed; and out of it came a reek so foul, and a sense of lurking malice so intense, that Frodo reeled. And at that moment Sam too lurched and fell forwards.

Fighting off both the sickness and the fear, Frodo gripped Sam's hand. 'Up!' he said in a hoarse breath without voice. 'It all comes from here, the stench and the peril. Now for it! Quick!'

Calling up his remaining strength and resolution, he dragged Sam to his feet, and forced his own limbs to move.

Sam stumbled beside him. One step, two steps, three steps – at last six steps. Maybe they had passed the dreadful unseen opening, but whether that was so or not, suddenly it was easier to move, as if some hostile will for the moment had released them. They struggled on, still hand in hand.

But almost at once they came to a new difficulty. The tunnel forked, or so it seemed, and in the dark they could not tell which was the wider way, or which kept nearer to the straight. Which should they take, the left, or the right? They knew of nothing to guide them, yet a false choice would almost certainly be fatal.

'Which way has Gollum gone?' panted Sam. 'And why didn't he wait?'

'Sméagol!' said Frodo, trying to call. 'Sméagol!' But his voice croaked, and the name fell dead almost as it left his lips. There was no answer, not an echo, not even a tremor of the air.

'He's really gone this time, I fancy,' muttered Sam. 'I guess this is just exactly where he meant to bring us. Gollum! If ever I lay hands on you again, you'll be sorry for it.'

Presently, groping and fumbling in the dark, they found that the opening on the left was blocked: either it was a blind, or else some great stone had fallen in the passage. 'This can't be the way,' Frodo whispered. 'Right or wrong, we must take the other.'

'And quick!' Sam panted. 'There's something worse than Gollum about. I can feel something looking at us.'

They had not gone more than a few yards when from behind them came a sound, startling and horrible in the heavy padded silence: a gurgling, bubbling noise, and a long venomous hiss. They wheeled round, but nothing could be seen. Still as stones they stood, staring, waiting for they did not know what.

'It's a trap!' said Sam, and he laid his hand upon the hilt of his sword; and as he did so, he thought of the darkness of the barrow whence it came. 'I wish old Tom was near us now!' he thought. Then, as he stood, darkness about him

and a blackness of despair and anger in his heart, it seemed
to him that he saw a light: a light in his mind, almost unbearably bright at first, as a sun-ray to the eyes of one long hidden
in a windowless pit. Then the light became colour: green,
gold, silver, white. Far off, as in a little picture drawn by
elven-fingers, he saw the Lady Galadriel standing on the
grass in Lórien, and gifts were in her hands. *And you, Ring-
bearer*, he heard her say, remote but clear, *for you I have
prepared this.*

The bubbling hiss drew nearer, and there was a creaking
as of some great jointed thing that moved with slow purpose
in the dark. A reek came on before it. 'Master, master!' cried
Sam, and life and urgency came back into his voice. 'The
Lady's gift! The star-glass! A light to you in dark places, she
said it was to be. The star-glass!'

'The star-glass?' muttered Frodo, as one answering out of
sleep, hardly comprehending. 'Why yes! Why had I forgotten
it? *A light when all other lights go out!* And now indeed light
alone can help us.'

Slowly his hand went to his bosom, and slowly he held
aloft the Phial of Galadriel. For a moment it glimmered, faint
as a rising star struggling in heavy earthward mists, and then
as its power waxed, and hope grew in Frodo's mind, it began
to burn, and kindled to a silver flame, a minute heart of
dazzling light, as though Eärendil had himself come down
from the high sunset paths with the last Silmaril upon his
brow. The darkness receded from it, until it seemed to shine
in the centre of a globe of airy crystal, and the hand that held
it sparkled with white fire.

Frodo gazed in wonder at this marvellous gift that he had
so long carried, not guessing its full worth and potency. Seldom had he remembered it on the road, until they came to
Morgul Vale, and never had he used it for fear of its revealing
light. *Aiya Eärendil Elenion Ancalima!* he cried, and knew not
what he had spoken; for it seemed that another voice spoke
through his, clear, untroubled by the foul air of the pit.

But other potencies there are in Middle-earth, powers of night, and they are old and strong. And She that walked in the darkness had heard the Elves cry that cry far back in the deeps of time, and she had not heeded it, and it did not daunt her now. Even as Frodo spoke he felt a great malice bent upon him, and a deadly regard considering him. Not far down the tunnel, between them and the opening where they had reeled and stumbled, he was aware of eyes growing visible, two great clusters of many-windowed eyes – the coming menace was unmasked at last. The radiance of the star-glass was broken and thrown back from their thousand facets, but behind the glitter a pale deadly fire began steadily to glow within, a flame kindled in some deep pit of evil thought. Monstrous and abominable eyes they were, bestial and yet filled with purpose and with hideous delight, gloating over their prey trapped beyond all hope of escape.

Frodo and Sam, horror-stricken, began slowly to back away, their own gaze held by the dreadful stare of those baleful eyes; but as they backed so the eyes advanced. Frodo's hand wavered, and slowly the Phial drooped. Then suddenly, released from the holding spell to run a little while in vain panic for the amusement of the eyes, they both turned and fled together; but even as they ran Frodo looked back and saw with terror that at once the eyes came leaping up behind. The stench of death was like a cloud about him.

'Stand! stand!' he cried desperately. 'Running is no use.'

Slowly the eyes crept nearer.

'Galadriel!' he called, and gathering his courage he lifted up the Phial once more. The eyes halted. For a moment their regard relaxed, as if some hint of doubt troubled them. Then Frodo's heart flamed within him, and without thinking what he did, whether it was folly or despair or courage, he took the Phial in his left hand, and with his right hand drew his sword. Sting flashed out, and the sharp elven-blade sparkled in the silver light, but at its edges a blue fire flicked. Then holding the star aloft and the bright sword advanced,

Frodo, hobbit of the Shire, walked steadily down to meet the eyes.

They wavered. Doubt came into them as the light approached. One by one they dimmed, and slowly they drew back. No brightness so deadly had ever afflicted them before. From sun and moon and star they had been safe underground, but now a star had descended into the very earth. Still it approached, and the eyes began to quail. One by one they all went dark; they turned away, and a great bulk, beyond the light's reach, heaved its huge shadow in between. They were gone.

'Master, master!' cried Sam. He was close behind, his own sword drawn and ready. 'Stars and glory! But the Elves would make a song of that, if ever they heard of it! And may I live to tell them and hear them sing. But don't go on, master! Don't go down to that den! Now's our only chance. Now let's get out of this foul hole!'

And so back they turned once more, first walking and then running; for as they went the floor of the tunnel rose steeply, and with every stride they climbed higher above the stenches of the unseen lair, and strength returned to limb and heart. But still the hatred of the Watcher lurked behind them, blind for a while, perhaps, but undefeated, still bent on death. And now there came a flow of air to meet them, cold and thin. The opening, the tunnel's end, at last it was before them. Panting, yearning for a roofless place, they flung themselves forward; and then in amazement they staggered, tumbling back. The outlet was blocked with some barrier, but not of stone: soft and a little yielding it seemed, and yet strong and impervious; air filtered through, but not a glimmer of any light. Once more they charged and were hurled back.

Holding aloft the Phial Frodo looked and before him he saw a greyness which the radiance of the star-glass did not pierce and did not illuminate, as if it were a shadow that being cast by no light, no light could dissipate. Across the width and height of the tunnel a vast web was spun, orderly as the web of some huge spider, but denser-woven and far greater, and each thread was as thick as rope.

Sam laughed grimly. 'Cobwebs!' he said. 'Is that all? Cobwebs! But what a spider! Have at 'em, down with 'em!'

In a fury he hewed at them with his sword, but the thread that he struck did not break. It gave a little and then sprang back like a plucked bowstring, turning the blade and tossing up both sword and arm. Three times Sam struck with all his force, and at last one single cord of all the countless cords snapped and twisted, curling and whipping through the air. One end of it lashed Sam's hand, and he cried out in pain, starting back and drawing his hand across his mouth.

'It will take days to clear the road like this,' he said. 'What's to be done? Have those eyes come back?'

'No, not to be seen,' said Frodo. 'But I still feel that they are looking at me, or thinking about me: making some other plan, perhaps. If this light were lowered, or if it failed, they would quickly come again.'

'Trapped in the end!' said Sam bitterly, his anger rising again above weariness and despair. 'Gnats in a net. May the curse of Faramir bite that Gollum and bite him quick!'

'That would not help us now,' said Frodo. 'Come! Let us see what Sting can do. It is an elven-blade. There were webs of horror in the dark ravines of Beleriand where it was forged. But you must be the guard and hold back the eyes. Here, take the star-glass. Do not be afraid. Hold it up and watch!'

Then Frodo stepped up to the great grey net, and hewed it with a wide sweeping stroke, drawing the bitter edge swiftly across a ladder of close-strung cords, and at once springing away. The blue-gleaming blade shore through them like a scythe through grass, and they leaped and writhed and then hung loose. A great rent was made.

Stroke after stroke he dealt, until at last all the web within his reach was shattered, and the upper portion blew and swayed like a loose veil in the incoming wind. The trap was broken.

'Come!' cried Frodo. 'On! On!' Wild joy at their escape from the very mouth of despair suddenly filled all his mind. His head whirled as with a draught of potent wine. He sprang out, shouting as he came.

It seemed light in that dark land to his eyes that had passed through the den of night. The great smokes had risen and grown thinner, and the last hours of a sombre day were passing; the red glare of Mordor had died away in sullen gloom. Yet it seemed to Frodo that he looked upon a morning of sudden hope. Almost he had reached the summit of the wall. Only a little higher now. The Cleft, Cirith Ungol, was before him, a dim notch in the black ridge, and the horns of rock darkling in the sky on either side. A short race, a sprinter's course, and he would be through!

'The pass, Sam!' he cried, not heeding the shrillness of his voice, that released from the choking airs of the tunnel rang out now high and wild. 'The pass! Run, run, and we'll be through – through before any one can stop us!'

Sam came up behind as fast as he could urge his legs; but glad as he was to be free, he was uneasy, and as he ran, he kept on glancing back at the dark arch of the tunnel, fearing to see eyes, or some shape beyond his imagining, spring out in pursuit. Too little did he or his master know of the craft of Shelob. She had many exits from her lair.

There agelong she had dwelt, an evil thing in spider-form, even such as once of old had lived in the Land of the Elves in the West that is now under the Sea, such as Beren fought in the Mountains of Terror in Doriath, and so came to Lúthien upon the green sward amid the hemlocks in the moonlight long ago. How Shelob came there, flying from ruin, no tale tells, for out of the Dark Years few tales have come. But still she was there, who was there before Sauron, and before the first stone of Barad-dûr; and she served none but herself, drinking the blood of Elves and Men, bloated and grown fat with endless brooding on her feasts, weaving webs of shadow; for all living things were her food, and her vomit darkness. Far and wide her lesser broods, bastards of the miserable mates, her own offspring, that she slew, spread from glen to glen, from the Ephel Dúath to the eastern hills, to Dol Guldur and the fastnesses of Mirkwood. But none could rival her, Shelob the Great, last child of Ungoliant to trouble the unhappy world.

Already, years before, Gollum had beheld her, Sméagol who pried into all dark holes, and in past days he had bowed and worshipped her, and the darkness of her evil will walked through all the ways of his weariness beside him, cutting him off from light and from regret. And he had promised to bring her food. But her lust was not his lust. Little she knew of or cared for towers, or rings, or anything devised by mind or hand, who only desired death for all others, mind and body, and for herself a glut of life, alone, swollen till the mountains could no longer hold her up and the darkness could not contain her.

But that desire was yet far away, and long now had she been hungry, lurking in her den, while the power of Sauron grew, and light and living things forsook his borders; and the city in the valley was dead, and no Elf or Man came near, only the unhappy Orcs. Poor food and wary. But she must eat, and however busily they delved new winding passages from the pass and from their tower, ever she found some way to snare them. But she lusted for sweeter meat. And Gollum had brought it to her.

'We'll see, we'll see,' he said often to himself, when the evil mood was on him, as he walked the dangerous road from Emyn Muil to Morgul Vale, 'we'll see. It may well be, O yes, it may well be that when She throws away the bones and the empty garments, we shall find it, we shall get it, the Precious, a reward for poor Sméagol who brings nice food. And we'll save the Precious, as we promised. O yes. And when we've got it safe, then She'll know it, O yes, then we'll pay Her back, my precious. Then we'll pay everyone back!'

So he thought in an inner chamber of his cunning, which he still hoped to hide from her, even when he had come to her again and had bowed low before her while his companions slept.

And as for Sauron: he knew where she lurked. It pleased him that she should dwell there hungry but unabated in malice, a more sure watch upon that ancient path into his land than any other that his skill could have devised. And Orcs, they were useful slaves, but he had them in plenty. If now and again Shelob caught them to stay her appetite, she was welcome: he could spare them. And sometimes as a man may cast a dainty to his cat (*his cat* he calls her, but she owns him not) Sauron would send her prisoners that he had no better uses for: he would have them driven to her hole, and report brought back to him of the play she made.

So they both lived, delighting in their own devices, and feared no assault, nor wrath, nor any end of their wickedness. Never yet had any fly escaped from Shelob's webs, and the greater now was her rage and hunger.

But nothing of this evil which they had stirred up against them did poor Sam know, except that a fear was growing on him, a menace which he could not see; and such a weight did it become that it was a burden to him to run, and his feet seemed leaden.

Dread was round him, and enemies before him in the pass, and his master was in a fey mood running heedlessly to meet them. Turning his eyes away from the shadow behind and the deep gloom beneath the cliff upon his left, he looked ahead, and he saw two things that increased his dismay. He saw that the sword which Frodo still held unsheathed was glittering with blue flame; and he saw that though the sky behind was now dark, still the window in the tower was glowing red.

'Orcs!' he muttered. 'We'll never rush it like this. There's Orcs about, and worse than Orcs.' Then returning quickly to his long habit of secrecy, he closed his hand about the precious Phial which he still bore. Red with his own living blood his hand shone for a moment, and then he thrust the revealing light deep into a pocket near his breast and drew his elven-cloak about him. Now he tried to quicken his pace. His master was gaining on him; already he was some twenty strides ahead, flitting on like a shadow; soon he would be lost to sight in that grey world.

Hardly had Sam hidden the light of the star-glass when she came. A little way ahead and to his left he saw suddenly, issuing from a black hole of shadow under the cliff, the most loathly shape that he had ever beheld, horrible beyond the horror of an evil dream. Most like a spider she was, but huger than the great hunting beasts, and more terrible than they because of the evil purpose in her remorseless eyes. Those same eyes that he had thought daunted and defeated, there they were lit with a fell light again, clustering in her out-thrust head. Great horns she had, and behind her short stalk-like neck was her huge swollen body, a vast bloated bag, swaying and sagging between her legs; its great bulk was black, blotched with livid marks, but the belly underneath was pale and luminous and gave forth a stench. Her legs were bent, with great knobbed joints high above her back, and hairs that stuck out like steel spines, and at each leg's end there was a claw.

As soon as she had squeezed her soft squelching body and its folded limbs out of the upper exit from her lair, she moved with a horrible speed, now running on her creaking legs, now making a sudden bound. She was between Sam and his master. Either she did not see Sam, or she avoided him for the moment as the bearer of the light, and fixed all her intent upon one prey, upon Frodo, bereft of his Phial, running heedless up the path, unaware yet of his peril. Swiftly he ran, but Shelob was swifter; in a few leaps she would have him.

Sam gasped and gathered all his remaining breath to shout. 'Look out behind!' he yelled. 'Look out, master! I'm' – but suddenly his cry was stifled.

A long clammy hand went over his mouth and another caught him by the neck, while something wrapped itself about his leg. Taken off his guard he toppled backwards into the arms of his attacker.

'Got him!' hissed Gollum in his ear. 'At last, my precious, we've got him, yes, the nassty hobbit. We takes this one. She'll get the other. O yes, Shelob will get him, not Sméagol: he promised; he won't hurt Master at all. But he's got you, you nassty filthy little sneak!' He spat on Sam's neck.

Fury at the treachery, and desperation at the delay when his master was in deadly peril, gave to Sam a sudden violence and strength that was far beyond anything that Gollum had expected from this slow stupid hobbit, as he thought him. Not Gollum himself could have twisted more quickly or more fiercely. His hold on Sam's mouth slipped, and Sam ducked and lunged forward again, trying to tear away from the grip on his neck. His sword was still in his hand, and on his left arm, hanging by its thong, was Faramir's staff. Desperately he tried to turn and stab his enemy. But Gollum was too quick. His long right arm shot out, and he grabbed Sam's wrist: his fingers were like a vice; slowly and relentlessly he bent the hand down and forward, till with a cry of pain Sam released the sword and it fell to the ground; and all the while Gollum's other hand was tightening on Sam's throat.

Then Sam played his last trick. With all his strength he pulled away and got his feet firmly planted; then suddenly he drove his legs against the ground and with his whole force hurled himself backwards.

Not expecting even this simple trick from Sam, Gollum fell over with Sam on top, and he received the weight of the sturdy hobbit in his stomach. A sharp hiss came out of him, and for a second his hand upon Sam's throat loosened; but his fingers still gripped the sword-hand. Sam tore himself forward and away, and stood up, and then quickly he wheeled away to his right, pivoted on the wrist held by Gollum. Laying hold of the staff with his left hand, Sam swung it up, and down it came with a whistling crack on Gollum's outstretched arm, just below the elbow.

With a squeal Gollum let go. Then Sam waded in; not

waiting to change the staff from left to right he dealt another savage blow. Quick as a snake Gollum slithered aside, and the stroke aimed at his head fell across his back. The staff cracked and broke. That was enough for him. Grabbing from behind was an old game of his, and seldom had he failed in it. But this time, misled by spite, he had made the mistake of speaking and gloating before he had both hands on his victim's neck. Everything had gone wrong with his beautiful plan, since that horrible light had so unexpectedly appeared in the darkness. And now he was face to face with a furious enemy, little less than his own size. This fight was not for him. Sam swept up his sword from the ground and raised it. Gollum squealed, and springing aside on to all fours, he jumped away in one big bound like a frog. Before Sam could reach him, he was off, running with amazing speed back towards the tunnel.

Sword in hand Sam went after him. For the moment he had forgotten everything else but the red fury in his brain and the desire to kill Gollum. But before he could overtake him, Gollum was gone. Then as the dark hole stood before him and the stench came out to meet him, like a clap of thunder the thought of Frodo and the monster smote upon Sam's mind. He spun round, and rushed wildly up the path, calling and calling his master's name. He was too late. So far Gollum's plot had succeeded.

CHAPTER X

THE CHOICES OF MASTER SAMWISE

Frodo was lying face upward on the ground and the monster was bending over him, so intent upon her victim that she took no heed of Sam and his cries, until he was close at hand. As he rushed up he saw that Frodo was already bound in cords, wound about him from ankle to shoulder, and the monster with her great forelegs was beginning half to lift, half to drag his body away.

On the near side of him lay, gleaming on the ground, his elven-blade, where it had fallen useless from his grasp. Sam did not wait to wonder what was to be done, or whether he was brave, or loyal, or filled with rage. He sprang forward with a yell, and seized his master's sword in his left hand. Then he charged. No onslaught more fierce was ever seen in the savage world of beasts, where some desperate small creature armed with little teeth, alone, will spring upon a tower of horn and hide that stands above its fallen mate.

Disturbed as if out of some gloating dream by his small yell she turned slowly the dreadful malice of her glance upon him. But almost before she was aware that a fury was upon her greater than any she had known in countless years, the shining sword bit upon her foot and shore away the claw. Sam sprang in, inside the arches of her legs, and with a quick upthrust of his other hand stabbed at the clustered eyes upon her lowered head. One great eye went dark.

Now the miserable creature was right under her, for the moment out of the reach of her sting and of her claws. Her vast belly was above him with its putrid light, and the stench of it almost smote him down. Still his fury held for one more blow, and before she could sink upon him, smothering him and all his little impudence of courage, he slashed the bright elven-blade across her with desperate strength.

But Shelob was not as dragons are, no softer spot had she save only her eyes. Knobbed and pitted with corruption was her age-old hide, but ever thickened from within with layer on layer of evil growth. The blade scored it with a dreadful gash, but those hideous folds could not be pierced by any strength of men, not though Elf or Dwarf should forge the steel or the hand of Beren or of Túrin wield it. She yielded to the stroke, and then heaved up the great bag of her belly high above Sam's head. Poison frothed and bubbled from the wound. Now splaying her legs she drove her huge bulk down on him again. Too soon. For Sam still stood upon his feet, and dropping his own sword, with both hands he held the elven-blade point upwards, fending off that ghastly roof; and so Shelob, with the driving force of her own cruel will, with strength greater than any warrior's hand, thrust herself upon a bitter spike. Deep, deep it pricked, as Sam was crushed slowly to the ground.

No such anguish had Shelob ever known, or dreamed of knowing, in all her long world of wickedness. Not the doughtiest soldier of old Gondor, nor the most savage Orc entrapped, had ever thus endured her, or set blade to her beloved flesh. A shudder went through her. Heaving up again, wrenching away from the pain, she bent her writhing limbs beneath her and sprang backwards in a convulsive leap.

Sam had fallen to his knees by Frodo's head, his senses reeling in the foul stench, his two hands still gripping the hilt of the sword. Through the mist before his eyes he was aware dimly of Frodo's face, and stubbornly he fought to master himself and to drag himself out of the swoon that was upon him. Slowly he raised his head and saw her, only a few paces away, eyeing him, her beak drabbling a spittle of venom, and a green ooze trickling from below her wounded eye. There she crouched, her shuddering belly splayed upon the ground, the great bows of her legs quivering, as she gathered herself for another spring – this time to crush and sting to death:

no little bite of poison to still the struggling of her meat; this time to slay and then to rend.

Even as Sam himself crouched, looking at her, seeing his death in her eyes, a thought came to him, as if some remote voice had spoken, and he fumbled in his breast with his left hand, and found what he sought: cold and hard and solid it seemed to his touch in a phantom world of horror, the Phial of Galadriel.

'Galadriel!' he said faintly, and then he heard voices far off but clear: the crying of the Elves as they walked under the stars in the beloved shadows of the Shire, and the music of the Elves as it came through his sleep in the Hall of Fire in the house of Elrond.

Gilthoniel A Elbereth!

And then his tongue was loosed and his voice cried in a language which he did not know:

> *A Elbereth Gilthoniel*
> *o menel palan-diriel,*
> *le nallon sí di'nguruthos!*
> *A tiro nin, Fanuilos!*

And with that he staggered to his feet and was Samwise the hobbit, Hamfast's son, again.

'Now come, you filth!' he cried. 'You've hurt my master, you brute, and you'll pay for it. We're going on; but we'll settle with you first. Come on, and taste it again!'

As if his indomitable spirit had set its potency in motion, the glass blazed suddenly like a white torch in his hand. It flamed like a star that leaping from the firmament sears the dark air with intolerable light. No such terror out of heaven had ever burned in Shelob's face before. The beams of it entered into her wounded head and scored it with unbearable pain, and the dreadful infection of light spread from eye to eye. She fell back beating the air with her forelegs, her sight

blasted by inner lightnings, her mind in agony. Then turning her maimed head away, she rolled aside and began to
crawl, claw by claw, towards the opening in the dark cliff
behind.

Sam came on. He was reeling like a drunken man, but he
came on. And Shelob cowed at last, shrunken in defeat, jerked
and quivered as she tried to hasten from him. She reached
the hole, and squeezing down, leaving a trail of green-yellow
slime, she slipped in, even as Sam hewed a last stroke at her
dragging legs. Then he fell to the ground.

Shelob was gone; and whether she lay long in her lair,
nursing her malice and her misery, and in slow years of
darkness healed herself from within, rebuilding her clustered
eyes, until with hunger like death she spun once more her
dreadful snares in the glens of the Mountains of Shadow,
this tale does not tell.

Sam was left alone. Wearily, as the evening of the Nameless
Land fell upon the place of battle, he crawled back to his
master.

'Master, dear master,' he said, but Frodo did not speak.
As he had run forward, eager, rejoicing to be free, Shelob
with hideous speed had come behind and with one swift
stroke had stung him in the neck. He lay now pale, and heard
no voice, and did not move.

'Master, dear master!' said Sam, and through a long silence
waited, listening in vain.

Then as quickly as he could he cut away the binding cords
and laid his head upon Frodo's breast and to his mouth, but
no stir of life could he find, nor feel the faintest flutter of the
heart. Often he chafed his master's hands and feet, and
touched his brow, but all were cold.

'Frodo, Mr. Frodo!' he called. 'Don't leave me here alone!
It's your Sam calling. Don't go where I can't follow! Wake
up, Mr. Frodo! O wake up, Frodo, me dear, me dear. Wake
up!'

⋆   ⋆   ⋆

Then anger surged over him, and he ran about his master's body in a rage, stabbing the air, and smiting the stones, and shouting challenges. Presently he came back, and bending looked at Frodo's face, pale beneath him in the dusk. And suddenly he saw that he was in the picture that was revealed to him in the mirror of Galadriel in Lórien: Frodo with a pale face lying fast asleep under a great dark cliff. Or fast asleep he had thought then. 'He's dead!' he said. 'Not asleep, dead!' And as he said it, as if the words had set the venom to its work again, it seemed to him that the hue of the face grew livid green.

And then black despair came down on him, and Sam bowed to the ground, and drew his grey hood over his head, and night came into his heart, and he knew no more.

When at last the blackness passed, Sam looked up and shadows were about him; but for how many minutes or hours the world had gone dragging on he could not tell. He was still in the same place, and still his master lay beside him dead. The mountains had not crumbled nor the earth fallen into ruin.

'What shall I do, what shall I do?' he said. 'Did I come all this way with him for nothing?' And then he remembered his own voice speaking words that at the time he did not understand himself, at the beginning of their journey: *I have something to do before the end. I must see it through, sir, if you understand.*

'But what can I do? Not leave Mr. Frodo dead, unburied on the top of the mountains, and go home? Or go on? Go on?' he repeated, and for a moment doubt and fear shook him. 'Go on? Is that what I've got to do? And leave him?'

Then at last he began to weep; and going to Frodo he composed his body, and folded his cold hands upon his breast, and wrapped his cloak about him; and he laid his own sword at one side, and the staff that Faramir had given at the other.

'If I'm to go on,' he said, 'then I must take your sword,

by your leave, Mr. Frodo, but I'll put this one to lie by you, as it lay by the old king in the barrow; and you've got your beautiful mithril coat from old Mr. Bilbo. And your star-glass, Mr. Frodo, you did lend it to me and I'll need it, for I'll be always in the dark now. It's too good for me, and the Lady gave it to you, but maybe she'd understand. Do *you* under-stand, Mr. Frodo? I've got to go on.'

But he could not go, not yet. He knelt and held Frodo's hand and could not release it. And time went by and still he knelt, holding his master's hand, and in his heart keeping a debate.

Now he tried to find strength to tear himself away and go on a lonely journey – for vengeance. If once he could go, his anger would bear him down all the roads of the world, pursu-ing, until he had him at last: Gollum. Then Gollum would die in a corner. But that was not what he had set out to do. It would not be worth while to leave his master for that. It would not bring him back. Nothing would. They had better both be dead together. And that too would be a lonely journey.

He looked on the bright point of the sword. He thought of the places behind where there was a black brink and an empty fall into nothingness. There was no escape that way. That was to do nothing, not even to grieve. That was not what he had set out to do. 'What am I to do then?' he cried again, and now he seemed plainly to know the hard answer: *see it through*. Another lonely journey, and the worst.

'What? Me, alone, go to the Crack of Doom and all?' He quailed still, but the resolve grew. 'What? *Me* take the Ring from *him*? The Council gave it to him.'

But the answer came at once: 'And the Council gave him companions, so that the errand should not fail. And you are the last of all the Company. The errand must not fail.'

'I wish I wasn't the last,' he groaned. 'I wish old Gandalf was here, or somebody. Why am I left all alone to make up my mind? I'm sure to go wrong. And it's not for me to go taking the Ring, putting myself forward.'

'But you haven't put yourself forward; you've been put forward. And as for not being the right and proper person, why, Mr. Frodo wasn't, as you might say, nor Mr. Bilbo. They didn't choose themselves.'

'Ah well, I must make up my own mind. I will make it up. But I'll be sure to go wrong: that'd be Sam Gamgee all over.

'Let me see now: if we're found here, or Mr. Frodo's found, and that Thing's on him, well, the Enemy will get it. And that's the end of all of us, of Lórien, and Rivendell, and the Shire and all. And there's no time to lose, or it'll be the end anyway. The war's begun, and more than likely things are all going the Enemy's way already. No chance to go back with It and get advice or permission. No, it's sit here till they come and kill me over master's body, and gets It; or take It and go.' He drew a deep breath. 'Then take It, it is!'

He stooped. Very gently he undid the clasp at the neck and slipped his hand inside Frodo's tunic; then with his other hand raising the head, he kissed the cold forehead, and softly drew the chain over it. And then the head lay quietly back again in rest. No change came over the still face, and by that more than by all other tokens Sam was convinced at last that Frodo had died and laid aside the Quest.

'Good-bye, master, my dear!' he murmured. 'Forgive your Sam. He'll come back to this spot when the job's done – if he manages it. And then he'll not leave you again. Rest you quiet till I come; and may no foul creature come anigh you! And if the Lady could hear me and give me one wish, I would wish to come back and find you again. Good-bye!'

And then he bent his own neck and put the chain upon it, and at once his head was bowed to the ground with the weight of the Ring, as if a great stone had been strung on him. But slowly, as if the weight became less, or new strength grew in him, he raised his head, and then with a great effort got to his feet and found that he could walk and bear his burden. And for a moment he lifted up the Phial and looked down at his master, and the light burned gently now with the soft radiance of the evening-star in summer, and in that light Frodo's face was fair of hue again, pale but beautiful with an elvish beauty, as of one who has long passed the shadows. And with the bitter comfort of that last sight Sam turned and hid the light and stumbled on into the growing dark.

He had not far to go. The tunnel was some way behind; the Cleft a couple of hundred yards ahead, or less. The path was visible in the dusk, a deep rut worn in ages of passage, running now gently up in a long trough with cliffs on either side. The trough narrowed rapidly. Soon Sam came to a long flight of broad shallow steps. Now the orc-tower was right above him, frowning black, and in it the red eye glowed. Now he was hidden in the dark shadow under it. He was coming to the top of the steps and was in the Cleft at last.

'I've made up my mind,' he kept saying to himself. But he had not. Though he had done his best to think it out, what he was doing was altogether against the grain of his nature. 'Have I got it wrong?' he muttered. 'What ought I to have done?'

As the sheer sides of the Cleft closed about him, before he reached the actual summit, before he looked at last on the path descending into the Nameless Land, he turned. For a moment, motionless in intolerable doubt, he looked back. He could still see, like a small blot in the gathering gloom, the mouth of the tunnel; and he thought he could see or guess where Frodo lay. He fancied there was a glimmer on the ground down there, or perhaps it was some trick of his tears, as he peered out at that high stony place where all his life had fallen in ruin.

'If only I could have my wish, my one wish,' he sighed, 'to go back and find him!' Then at last he turned to the road in front and took a few steps: the heaviest and the most reluctant he had ever taken.

★   ★   ★

Only a few steps; and now only a few more and he would
be going down and would never see that high place again.
And then suddenly he heard cries and voices. He stood still
as stone. Orc-voices. They were behind him and before him.
A noise of tramping feet and harsh shouts: Orcs were coming
up to the Cleft from the far side, from some entry to the
tower, perhaps. Tramping feet and shouts behind. He
wheeled round. He saw small red lights, torches, winking
away below there as they issued from the tunnel. At last the
hunt was up. The red eye of the tower had not been blind.
He was caught.

Now the flicker of approaching torches and the clink of
steel ahead was very near. In a minute they would reach the
top and be on him. He had taken too long in making up his
mind, and now it was no good. How could he escape, or
save himself, or save the Ring? The Ring. He was not aware
of any thought or decision. He simply found himself drawing
out the chain and taking the Ring in his hand. The head of
the orc-company appeared in the Cleft right before him.
Then he put it on.

The world changed, and a single moment of time was filled
with an hour of thought. At once he was aware that hearing
was sharpened while sight was dimmed, but otherwise than
in Shelob's lair. All things about him now were not dark but
vague; while he himself was there in a grey hazy world, alone,
like a small black solid rock, and the Ring, weighing down
his left hand, was like an orb of hot gold. He did not feel
invisible at all, but horribly and uniquely visible; and he knew
that somewhere an Eye was searching for him.

He heard the crack of stone, and the murmur of water far
off in Morgul Vale; and down away under the rock the bubbling misery of Shelob, groping, lost in some blind passage;
and voices in the dungeons of the tower; and the cries of the
Orcs as they came out of the tunnel; and deafening, roaring
in his ears, the crash of the feet and the rending clamour of
the Orcs before him. He shrank against the cliff. But they

marched up like a phantom company, grey distorted figures in a mist, only dreams of fear with pale flames in their hands. And they passed him by. He cowered, trying to creep away into some cranny and to hide.

He listened. The Orcs from the tunnel and the others marching down had sighted one another, and both parties were now hurrying and shouting. He heard them both clearly, and he understood what they said. Perhaps the Ring gave understanding of tongues, or simply understanding, especially of the servants of Sauron its maker, so that if he gave heed, he understood and translated the thought to himself. Certainly the Ring had grown greatly in power as it approached the places of its forging; but one thing it did not confer, and that was courage. At present Sam still thought only of hiding, of lying low till all was quiet again; and he listened anxiously. He could not tell how near the voices were, the words seemed almost in his ears.

'Hola! Gorbag! What are you doing up here? Had enough of war already?'

'Orders, you lubber. And what are you doing, Shagrat? Tired of lurking up there? Thinking of coming down to fight?'

'Orders to you. I'm in command of this pass. So speak civil. What's your report?'

'Nothing.'

'Hai! hai! yoi!' A yell broke into the exchanges of the leaders. The Orcs lower down had suddenly seen something. They began to run. So did the others.

'Hai! Hola! Here's something! Lying right in the road. A spy, a spy!' There was a hoot of snarling horns and a babel of baying voices.

With a dreadful stroke Sam was wakened from his cowering mood. They had seen his master. What would they do? He had heard tales of the Orcs to make the blood run cold. It could not be borne. He sprang up. He flung the Quest and all his decisions away, and fear and doubt with them. He knew now where his place was and had been: at his master's side, though what he could do there was not clear. Back he ran down the steps, down the path towards Frodo.

'How many are there?' he thought. 'Thirty or forty from the tower at least, and a lot more than that from down below, I guess. How many can I kill before they get me? They'll see the flame of the sword, as soon as I draw it, and they'll get me sooner or later. I wonder if any song will ever mention it: How Samwise fell in the High Pass and made a wall of bodies round his master. No, no song. Of course not, for the Ring'll be found, and there'll be no more songs. I can't help it. My place is by Mr. Frodo. They must understand that – Elrond and the Council, and the great Lords and Ladies with all their wisdom. Their plans have gone wrong. I can't be their Ring-bearer. Not without Mr. Frodo.'

But the Orcs were out of his dim sight now. He had had no time to consider himself, but now he realized that he was weary, weary almost to exhaustion: his legs would not carry him as he wished. He was too slow. The path seemed miles long. Where had they all got to in the mist?

There they were again! A good way ahead still. A cluster of figures round something lying on the ground; a few seemed to be darting this way and that, bent like dogs on a trail. He tried to make a spurt.

'Come on, Sam!' he said, 'or you'll be too late again.' He loosened the sword in its sheath. In a minute he would draw it, and then——

There was a wild clamour, hooting and laughing, as something was lifted from the ground. 'Ya hoi! Ya harri hoi! Up! Up!'

Then a voice shouted: 'Now off! The quick way. Back to the Undergate! She'll not trouble us tonight by all the signs.' The whole band of orc-figures began to move. Four in the middle were carrying a body high on their shoulders. 'Ya hoi!'

*   *   *

They had taken Frodo's body. They were off. He could not catch them up. Still he laboured on. The Orcs reached the tunnel and were passing in. Those with the burden went first, and behind them there was a good deal of struggling and jostling. Sam came on. He drew the sword, a flicker of blue in his wavering hand, but they did not see it. Even as he came panting up, the last of them vanished into the black hole.

For a moment he stood, gasping, clutching his breast. Then he drew his sleeve across his face, wiping away the grime, and sweat, and tears. 'Curse the filth!' he said, and sprang after them into the darkness.

It no longer seemed very dark to him in the tunnel, rather it was as if he had stepped out of a thin mist into a heavier fog. His weariness was growing but his will hardened all the more. He thought he could see the light of torches a little way ahead, but try as he would, he could not catch them up. Orcs go fast in tunnels, and this tunnel they knew well; for in spite of Shelob they were forced to use it often as the swiftest way from the Dead City over the mountains. In what far-off time the main tunnel and the great round pit had been made, where Shelob had taken up her abode in ages past, they did not know; but many byways they had themselves delved about it on either side, so as to escape the lair in their goings to and fro on the business of their masters. Tonight they did not intend to go far down, but were hastening to find a side-passage that led back to their watch-tower on the cliff. Most of them were gleeful, delighted with what they had found and seen, and as they ran they gabbled and yammered after the fashion of their kind. Sam heard the noise of their harsh voices, flat and hard in the dead air, and he could distinguish two voices from among all the rest: they were louder, and nearer to him. The captains of the two parties seemed to be bringing up the rear, debating as they went.

*   *   *

'Can't you stop your rabble making such a racket, Shag-rat?' grunted the one. 'We don't want Shelob on us.'

'Go on, Gorbag! Yours are making more than half the noise,' said the other. 'But let the lads play! No need to worry about Shelob for a bit, I reckon. She's sat on a nail, it seems, and we shan't cry about that. Didn't you see: a nasty mess all the way back to that cursed crack of hers? If we've stopped it once, we've stopped it a hundred times. So let 'em laugh. And we've struck a bit of luck at last: got something that Lugbúrz wants.'

'Lugbúrz wants it, eh? What is it, d'you think? Elvish it looked to me, but undersized. What's the danger in a thing like that?'

'Don't know till we've had a look.'

'Oho! So they haven't told you what to expect? They don't tell us all they know, do they? Not by half. But they can make mistakes, even the Top Ones can.'

'Sh, Gorbag!' Shagrat's voice was lowered, so that even with his strangely sharpened hearing Sam could only just catch what was said. 'They may, but they've got eyes and ears everywhere; some among my lot, as like as not. But there's no doubt about it, they're troubled about something. The Nazgûl down below are, by your account; and Lugbúrz is too. Something nearly slipped.'

'Nearly, you say!' said Gorbag.

'All right,' said Shagrat, 'but we'll talk of that later. Wait till we get to the Under-way. There's a place there where we can talk a bit, while the lads go on.'

Shortly afterwards Sam saw the torches disappear. Then there was a rumbling noise, and just as he hurried up, a bump. As far as he could guess the Orcs had turned and gone into the very opening which Frodo and he had tried and found blocked. It was still blocked.

There seemed to be a great stone in the way, but the Orcs had got through somehow, for he could hear their voices on the other side. They were still running along, deeper and deeper into the mountain, back towards the tower. Sam felt desperate. They were carrying off his master's body for some foul purpose and he could not follow. He thrust and pushed at the block, and he threw himself against it, but it did not yield. Then not far inside, or so he thought, he heard the two captains' voices talking again. He stood still listening for a little, hoping perhaps to learn something useful. Perhaps Gorbag, who seemed to belong to Minas Morgul, would come out, and he could then slip in.

'No, I don't know,' said Gorbag's voice. 'The messages go through quicker than anything could fly, as a rule. But I don't enquire how it's done. Safest not to. Grr! Those Nazgûl give me the creeps. And they skin the body off you as soon as look at you, and leave you all cold in the dark on the other side. But He likes 'em; they're His favourites nowadays, so it's no use grumbling. I tell you, it's no game serving down in the city.'

'You should try being up here with Shelob for company,' said Shagrat.

'I'd like to try somewhere where there's none of 'em. But the war's on now, and when that's over things may be easier.'

'It's going well, they say.'

'They would,' grunted Gorbag. 'We'll see. But anyway, if it does go well, there should be a lot more room. What d'you say? – if we get a chance, you and me'll slip off and set up somewhere on our own with a few trusty lads, somewhere where there's good loot nice and handy, and no big bosses.'

'Ah!' said Shagrat. 'Like old times.'

'Yes,' said Gorbag. 'But don't count on it. I'm not easy in my mind. As I said, the Big Bosses, ay,' his voice sank almost to a whisper, 'ay, even the Biggest, can make mistakes. Something nearly slipped, you say. I say, something *has* slipped. And we've got to look out. Always the poor Uruks to put slips right, and small thanks. But don't forget: the enemies don't love us any more than they love Him, and if they get topsides on Him, we're done too. But see here: when were you ordered out?'

'About an hour ago, just before you saw us. A message

came: *Nazgûl uneasy. Spies feared on Stairs. Double vigilance. Patrol to head of Stairs.* I came at once.'

'Bad business,' said Gorbag. 'See here – our Silent Watchers were uneasy more than two days ago, that I know. But my patrol wasn't ordered out for another day, nor any message sent to Lugbúrz either: owing to the Great Signal going up, and the High Nazgûl going off to the war, and all that. And then they couldn't get Lugbúrz to pay attention for a good while, I'm told.'

'The Eye was busy elsewhere, I suppose,' said Shagrat. 'Big things going on away west, they say.'

'I daresay,' growled Gorbag. 'But in the meantime enemies have got up the Stairs. And what were you up to? You're supposed to keep watch, aren't you, special orders or no? What are you for?'

'That's enough! Don't try and teach me my job. We were awake all right. We knew there were funny things going on.'

'Very funny!'

'Yes, very funny: lights and shouting and all. But Shelob was on the go. My lads saw her and her Sneak.'

'Her Sneak? What's that?'

'You must have seen him: little thin black fellow; like a spider himself, or perhaps more like a starved frog. He's been here before. Came *out* of Lugbúrz the first time, years ago, and we had word from High Up to let him pass. He's been up the Stairs once or twice since then, but we've left him alone: seems to have some understanding with Her Ladyship. I suppose he's no good to eat: she wouldn't worry about words from High Up. But a fine guard you keep in the valley: he was up here a day before all this racket. Early last night we saw him. Anyway my lads reported that Her Ladyship was having some fun, and that seemed good enough for me, until the message came. I thought her Sneak had brought her a toy, or that you'd perhaps sent her a present, a prisoner of war or something. I don't interfere when she's playing. Nothing gets by Shelob when she's on the hunt.'

'Nothing, say you! Didn't you use your eyes back there?

I tell you I'm not easy in my mind. Whatever came up the Stairs, *did* get by. It cut her web and got clean out of the hole. That's something to think about!'

'Ah well, but she got him in the end, didn't she?'

'*Got* him? Got *who*? This little fellow? But if he was the only one, then she'd have had him off to her larder long before, and there he'd be now. And if Lugbúrz wanted him, *you'd* have to go and get him. Nice for you. But there was more than one.'

At this point Sam began to listen more attentively and pressed his ear against the stone.

'Who cut the cords she'd put round him, Shagrat? Same one as cut the web. Didn't you see that? And who stuck a pin into Her Ladyship? Same one, I reckon. And where is he? Where is he, Shagrat?'

Shagrat made no reply.

'You may well put your thinking cap on, if you've got one. It's no laughing matter. No one, *no* one has ever stuck a pin in Shelob before, as you should know well enough. There's no grief in that; but think – there's someone loose hereabouts as is more dangerous than any other damned rebel that ever walked since the bad old times, since the Great Siege. Something *has* slipped.'

'And what is it then?' growled Shagrat.

'By all the signs, Captain Shagrat, I'd say there's a large warrior loose, Elf most likely, with an elf-sword anyway, and an axe as well maybe; and he's loose in your bounds, too, and you've never spotted him. Very funny indeed!' Gorbag spat. Sam smiled grimly at this description of himself.

'Ah well, you always did take a gloomy view,' said Shagrat. 'You can read the signs how you like, but there may be other ways to explain them. Anyhow, I've got watchers at every point, and I'm going to deal with one thing at a time. When I've had a look at the fellow we *have* caught, then I'll begin to worry about something else.'

'It's my guess you won't find much in that little fellow,' said Gorbag. 'He may have had nothing to do with the real mischief. The big fellow with the sharp sword doesn't seem to have thought him worth much anyhow – just left him lying: regular elvish trick.'

'We'll see. Come on now! We've talked enough. Let's go and have a look at the prisoner!'

'What are you going to do with him? Don't forget I spotted him first. If there's any game, me and my lads must be in it.'

'Now, now,' growled Shagrat, 'I have my orders. And it's more than my belly's worth, or yours, to break 'em. *Any* trespasser found by the guard is to be held at the tower. Prisoner is to be stripped. Full description of every article, garment, weapon, letter, ring, or trinket is to be sent to Lugbúrz at once, and to Lugbúrz *only*. And the prisoner is to be kept safe and intact, under pain of death for every member of the guard, until He sends or comes Himself. That's plain enough, and that's what I'm going to do.'

'Stripped, eh?' said Gorbag. 'What, teeth, nails, hair, and all?'

'No, none of that. He's for Lugbúrz, I tell you. He's wanted safe and whole.'

'You'll find that difficult,' laughed Gorbag. 'He's nothing but carrion now. What Lugbúrz will do with such stuff I can't guess. He might as well go in the pot.'

'You fool,' snarled Shagrat. 'You've been talking very clever, but there's a lot you don't know, though most other folk do. You'll be for the pot or for Shelob, if you don't take care. Carrion! Is that all you know of Her Ladyship? When she binds with cords, she's after meat. She doesn't eat dead meat, nor suck cold blood. This fellow isn't dead!'

Sam reeled, clutching at the stone. He felt as if the whole dark world was turning upside down. So great was the shock that he almost swooned, but even as he fought to keep a hold on his senses, deep inside him he was aware of the comment: 'You fool, he isn't dead, and your heart knew it. Don't trust your head, Samwise, it is not the best part of you. The trouble with you is that you never really had any hope. Now what is to be done?' For the moment nothing, but to prop himself against the unmoving stone and listen, listen to the vile orc-voices.

'Garn!' said Shagrat. 'She's got more than one poison. When she's hunting, she just gives 'em a dab in the neck and they go as limp as boned fish, and then she has her way with them. D'you remember old Ufthak? We lost him for days. Then we found him in a corner; hanging up he was, but he was wide awake and glaring. How we laughed! She'd forgotten him, maybe, but we didn't touch him – no good interfering with Her. Nar – this little filth, he'll wake up, in a few hours; and beyond feeling a bit sick for a bit, he'll be all right. Or would be, if Lugbúrz would let him alone. And of course, beyond wondering where he is and what's happened to him.'

'And what's going to happen to him,' laughed Gorbag. 'We can tell him a few stories at any rate, if we can't do anything else. I don't suppose he's ever been in lovely Lugbúrz, so he may like to know what to expect. This is going to be more funny than I thought. Let's go!'

'There's going to be no fun, I tell you,' said Shagrat. 'And he's got to be kept safe, or we're all as good as dead.'

'All right! But if I were you, I'd catch the big one that's loose, before you send in any report to Lugbúrz. It won't sound too pretty to say you've caught the kitten and let the cat escape.'

The voices began to move away. Sam heard the sound of feet receding. He was recovering from his shock, and now a wild fury was on him. 'I got it all wrong!' he cried. 'I knew I would. Now they've got him, the devils! the filth! Never leave your master, never, never: that was my right rule. And I knew it in my heart. May I be forgiven! Now I've got to get back to him. Somehow, somehow!'

He drew his sword again and beat on the stone with the hilt, but it only gave out a dull sound. The sword, however, blazed so brightly now that he could see dimly in its light. To his surprise he noticed that the great block was shaped like a heavy door, and was less than twice his own height. Above it was a dark blank space between the top and the low arch of the opening. It was probably only meant to be a stop against the intrusion of Shelob, fastened on the inside with some latch or bolt beyond the reach of her cunning. With his remaining strength Sam leaped and caught the top, scrambled up, and dropped; and then he ran madly, sword blazing in hand, round a bend and up a winding tunnel.

The news that his master was still alive roused him to a last effort beyond thought of weariness. He could not see anything ahead, for this new passage twisted and turned constantly; but he thought he was catching the two Orcs up: their voices were growing nearer again. Now they seemed quite close.

'That's what I'm going to do,' said Shagrat in angry tones. 'Put him right up in the top chamber.'

'What for?' growled Gorbag. 'Haven't you any lock-ups down below?'

'He's going out of harm's way, I tell you,' answered Shagrat. 'See? He's precious. I don't trust all my lads, and none of yours; nor you neither, when you're mad for fun. He's going where I want him, and where you won't come, if you don't keep civil. Up to the top, I say. He'll be safe there.'

'Will he?' said Sam. 'You're forgetting the great big elvish warrior that's loose!' And with that he raced round the last corner, only to find that by some trick of the tunnel, or of the hearing which the Ring gave him, he had misjudged the distance.

The two orc-figures were still some way ahead. He could see them now, black and squat against a red glare. The passage ran straight at last, up an incline; and at the end, wide open, were great double doors, leading probably to deep chambers far below the high horn of the tower. Already the

Orcs with their burden had passed inside. Gorbag and Shagrat were drawing near the gate.

Sam heard a burst of hoarse singing, blaring of horns and banging of gongs, a hideous clamour. Gorbag and Shagrat were already on the threshold.

Sam yelled and brandished Sting, but his little voice was drowned in the tumult. No one heeded him.

The great doors slammed to. Boom. The bars of iron fell into place inside. Clang. The gate was shut. Sam hurled himself against the bolted brazen plates and fell senseless to the ground. He was out in the darkness. Frodo was alive but taken by the Enemy.